Joey the Motor Home Mouse

JOEY
—the—
MOTOR HOME MOUSE

Jack E. Tetirick

iUniverse, Inc.
Bloomington

Joey the Motor Home Mouse

iUniverse books may be ordered through booksellers or by contacting:

iUniverse
1663 Liberty Drive
Bloomington, IN 47403
www.iuniverse.com
1-800-Authors (1-800-288-4677)

ISBN: 978-1-4759-3703-9 (sc)
ISBN: 978-1-4759-3702-2 (hc)
ISBN: 978-1-4759-3704-6 (e)

Library of Congress Control Number: 2012912195

Printed in the United States of America

iUniverse rev. date: 07/20/2012

This book is dedicated to Jesse. After all, it *was* his idea.

Contents

Foreword:

Instructions for the Use of This Book

Young children are not permitted to read this book by themselves. There are too many big words and too many situations that will need to be explained.

This book is to be read by adults and teenagers to *very smart* younger children only. Every difficult word must be defined, and every situation must be explained to the satisfaction of the child.

The only exception to this rule is that a child may read this book aloud in a classroom setting, where other children may comment, ask about unfamiliar words, and explain situations. In these settings, the teacher shall remain silent unless a disagreement arises about the meaning of something, in which case the teacher shall act as the final authority.

Under no circumstances are adults or teenagers permitted to read this book to themselves. This is simply for their own benefit; if another person is watching an adult or teen read this book from a distance and the reader is giggling or moving his or her lips silently or attempting to speak mouse, then the observer will think the reader is quite dippy, if you know what I mean.

The Author

Hey! Who are you?

        How did you get in here?

                What's your name?

                        Do you speak *mouse*?

Meet a few of Joey's special friends.

Adventure Number 1:

Joey Is Born

It was a dark and stormy night when Joey was born. Thunderclouds billowed in the blackness, and jagged streaks of lightning ignited; then the roar of thunder was heard, followed by silence—except for the swishing of windswept rain. Joey was the eighth little mouse out of a litter of nine, so you see, he very nearly missed being born at all—or at least not until the next time.

The thunder was so loud it could be heard inside the ball of paper and feathers that served as the mouse family's nest. The ball lay deep underneath a pile of loose straw that had been left, forgotten, in the corner of the barn.

The thunder actually shook the little ball with every blast, but Joey's mother only moved softly to make room for her newest baby. Little did she realize that this tiny little fellow was destined to be one of the greatest mice that ever lived: widely traveled, well educated, and as famous as any mouse could ever hope to be ... but that is information for further on in the story. For right now, he was just a little mouse, hungry and frightened. He didn't know it, but he was very happy that he didn't have to be famous or brave yet; all he had to do was wriggle in among his brothers and sisters to keep warm and to get something to eat. Which he did.

The storm raged on; the huge bolts of lightning raced across the sky and were quickly swallowed by huge claps of thunder. The rain continued in wavering sheets, smashing against the aged wood of the old barn, spraying through tiny cracks and clattering against the rusty metal roof.

At the far end of the barn, old Buck, a huge golden retriever, stood up and shook himself thoroughly. All of the noise irritated him. It was tough to be on guard duty with all of that noise! Anything could be going on! He shook again briefly and lay back down, but he kept an eye open, watching the flashes of lightning through the cracks in the sagging doors.

In the manger to the side, a feed trough was filled with stale hay, ignored now that there were no horses. In it was a much larger nest, one that would have filled a market basket—and *it* was filled with cats! Even in the very dim light, there peered five pairs of softly glowing orange-yellow eyes.

Billie Joe

This was Billie Joe's family: her daughter, Charlie, and her three grand-kittens, King, Fred, and Ruby.

Right now they weren't thinking about their names at all. They had missed their supper up at the farmhouse because of the rainstorm. They had had a dousing before they could scramble back to the nest, and after they crawled in, the hay had become all damp and sticky. They were, to be blunt about it, beginning to get into a bad mood.

Fred, the middle cat in the litter of Charlie's kittens, was the most adventurous. Even when he was in a bad mood, as he now was, he was very rarely mean about it; mostly he was just ornery, as he was about to be now.

Peering down through the dimness from the food trough, Fred could barely see Buck's big tail lying on the barn floor. It was a huge

King

tail, about the size of a baseball bat, except that it narrowed to a point at the end. Buck was very proud of his tail; he had seen it admired often and been told how beautiful it was. As a result, he waved it around a lot. Right now, though, the tail was lying quietly on the dusty floor and barely moving, except at the precious tip.

All in all, this was just too much for Fred to resist. He eased over the rough wooden edge of the food trough and coiled into a crouch. Then, in a great arching leap, he stretched across the gloom, landing squarely on the tail, giving it a quick nip and two lightning-fast raps with the claws of his left paw (Fred is left-handed). He then darted off to the side.

Buck

"*Arrough!*" went Buck, loud enough to shake the barn—if it had not already been shaking from the rainstorm. Buck leaped to his feet and spun around twice in a tight circle. "*Rrough!*" he said again, but not quite as loud because he had just seen Fred crouched in the corner. Buck took a big breath, almost like a sigh. "Doggone it, Fred, I wish you wouldn't jump on my tail like that, particularly when there is all of this noise outside, and I'm supposed to be guarding this barn!"

"From what?" asked Fred. He was still in a bad mood.

"Well," replied Buck, slightly puzzled, "from someone stealing something!"

"In this dump?" asked Fred.

Buck nodded, angling his head down toward a long stretch in the dimness, where there gleamed a beautiful motor home. He waved his tail twice to make certain it wasn't damaged. "Someone might try to steal that," he suggested.

"No way," countered Fred. "There's no gas in it, and the battery is dead. It takes your pal a week just to get it ready, remember?"

"Just the same," argued Buck, "that's my job, and I try to do it right. And you don't help a bit when you scare me like that. What if I had snapped at you and hurt you?"

"You're too slow, Buck," said Fred in a matter-of-fact tone. "You're big and you're tough, but where cats are concerned, you're too slow."

Fred's curiosity, like that of all cats, was easily aroused. So now he was interested in the monstrous machine, so silent in the dim light. He started to move down along it, placing each foot where the last one had landed to avoid raising the dust as much as was possible. Soon, he walked right past the mound of hay where the family of mice was wrapped tightly in its ball of feathers and soft fur.

In there, Joey was very, very young. Fred had not the slightest idea that, in the neglected pile of old straw, was his future best friend, a mouse who would later become a very famous mouse. In mouse time, which is how this story will be told, Joey was, at that moment, very close to zero.

Adventure Number 2:

Joey Meets (Some of) His Extended Family

It was a warm spring day when Joey began to learn about his larger family—cats, dogs, people, that sort of thing. His first encounter came very close to being a bad experience because it was still early in his mouse time, and he had not learned to always be very careful, especially in broad daylight.

Joey was working his way slowly along the edge of the barn floor. Joey's brothers and sisters had long since scattered from the nest, and he was feeling a bit lonely. The floor was covered with dry litter of all sorts—leaves left over from autumn, old straw, and several pignut hickory shells from the pignut hickory tree down by the farmhouse. Two squirrels, who were not very tidy, had scattered the shells all around after they had chewed the nuts open and eaten the insides. There was even an old oil can that the farmer had thrown across the barn when he cut his finger opening it. Joey was making far too much noise for a careful mouse as well as not paying attention—a common failing of short-lived mice. He happened to be looking up at the huge wheel well of the motor home. He saw his reflection in the bright chrome cover of the wheel and stood up on his hind legs to admire himself. Then he scurried under the motor home, tempted to see if he could find a way up inside—even though his mother had told him many times that he was *never* to go up in there, that there might be *mousetraps* in there.

Reluctantly, Joey turned around, but as he came out from under the edge of the motor home, he suddenly realized that he had just stumbled into a huge shadow that was *not right!* He looked up and saw the biggest cat he had ever seen, and *it was staring right at him!* Actually, it was the *only* cat he had ever seen, since he was just a bit over one mouse-year old. Of course, Joey had heard about cats; his aunts and uncles talked of little else as they gossiped underneath the straw, adding that the babies would learn about cats soon enough.

Fred

Well, thought Joey, *I guess this is it for me.*

"H-hello!" stammered Joey. He was so scared that it came out as a high squeak.

"Hi," replied the cat.

The tone sounded sort of friendly, but Joey was still scared. He couldn't help but notice it was a very handsome cat, sort of golden all over with some dark brown stripes and a not-altogether-unpleasant face. There were several cobwebs tangled in the cat's whiskers on the left side, which made him look silly.

"Wh-what are you doing here?" asked Joey.

"I am thinking about eating you," said the cat, but he didn't sound as if he really meant it.

There is one thing about Joey that he must have been born with: he was able to make up his mind about something, and when he did, he was very confident that he was right. He was always that way, even when he was very young. One mouse-year is very, very young—and most mice never get to be much older than that. The reason is mostly because they are so very tasty. They might as well be wearing a sign saying, *Genuine mouse! Delicious!*

"I don't think you want to eat me," announced Joey. To show his confidence, he stood up on his back legs and tried to look both friendly and self-confident. The morning sunlight cast a long shadow behind him.

Fred thought about this while staring at Joey. "No, I don't think I do either," he said. He then brightened with an idea. He twitched his whiskers, the ones with the tangle of cobwebs. Joey wanted to tell him about the cobwebs but decided this was the wrong time.

"Actually," continued Fred, "I don't like mouse to eat. I like canned food." Fred licked his lips, and the cobwebs bounced up and down. Fred must have seen Joey watching because, with a lightning-fast flick of a paw, he swept the cobwebs away.

Joey was beginning to realize how lucky he was.

"But don't you ever think, little fellow, even for a minute, that the other cats around here feel the same way! First of all, there are my sister and brother, Ruby and King. They're young, like me, but they are not *like* me, if you follow me. Understand?"

Joey looked around, wondering if they were there.

"Ruby looks like *me*," said Fred, trying to be helpful. "She is smaller, but King is a lot bigger. He is gray with very faint stripes. He is really very handsome; trouble is, he knows it." Fred sounded a bit jealous. "And then there's the ... dogs!" Fred had used a bad word.

"My mother said never to say words like that!" scolded Joey.

"I'm just trying to tell you about the—" Fred caught himself in time.

"Well, *go ahead!*" demanded Joey.

"There are three of them," announced Fred importantly. "You know Buck, of course, the big fellow who is so serious about guarding everything?"

7

Joey nodded. He had watched Buck from under the straw as he walked past the nest in the barn. Buck was always sniffing, and Joey was sure that Buck knew they were in there, but he didn't seem to mind. Joey even wondered if Buck couldn't smell at all and was just making a lot of sniffing noises.

"Then there's Lady," continued Fred. "She lives down in her own pen with her own water and food. It's all brand-new. Jack, the farmer, calls it a kennel."

Joey remembered wondering about that building that he had seen down a long lane leading away from the old barn.

"She's a *hunting dog!*" announced Fred. "Not mice, bigger things. She gets to ride around like royalty and be taken hunting; she even gets to go into the farmhouse to get a bath. She's sort of stuck-up, if you ask me."

Joey wanted to tell Fred that nobody had asked him, but, again, he thought it was not the right time.

"Then there's Sagebrush!" snapped Fred. "Let me tell you something, little fellow. You'd better look out for that sucker!"

"Why?" asked Joey.

"Why?" demanded Fred. "Because when he gets out down by the road where Jim, the policeman, lives, and that d— Well, that dog comes through here like a whirlwind, chasing the squirrels, catching groundhogs or anything else that's around, running cats up trees—he even snaps at them. You never know *what* that—that *dog* is going to do!" The bad word had popped out again. "He would make a snack out of you, fellow!" Fred was really getting worked up.

"And don't you trust my mom, either," cautioned Fred, looking guilty as he said it. "My mom is all gray and *very hard to see at night.* Some days she goes out, even when we don't need any food, and she hunts all night and brings all kinds of stuff home. *Ugh!* I hate it! I wish she wouldn't do that, but when I said so once, she told me that

8

if my grandmother, Billie Joe, hadn't been such a good hunter, we all would have frozen to death when those awful people dumped us out down on the road. Charlie, my mother, says our generation just doesn't appreciate how tough those times were then."

Joey was getting a bit bored with all of this, but he thought it was not the time to tell Fred.

Fred heard something that Joey did not. Fred glanced quickly behind them to the far end of the barn. "*Quick!*" he hissed, "*Get out of here! Billie Joe is coming!*"

Joey scrambled away in a panic, running and scratching deep underneath a pile of old boards. Fred hunched down beside the huge motor home. Through a crack, Joey watched the small cat approach where they had been standing. She walked with a very slow, soft step; everything seemed to be moving at once, in rhythm—her four feet seemed to be hardly touching the ground as she glided along the rough cement. Despite all the leaves and litter, she made hardly a sound. She swung her head from side to side as she walked, and she paused briefly to stare up into the wheel well of the motor home, sniffing the air briefly. She seemed so strong and powerful!

"Hi, Grandma!" said Fred, trying to sound pleasant, even though it was obvious he was frightened out of his wits. Of his own grandmother!

Billie Joe's glance swept over Fred like a bright green beacon and kept moving over to the spot against the wall where Joey had been standing. Fred shivered. "Grump!" he said softly under his breath, hardly louder than a thought.

Billie Joe's eyes snapped back onto Fred. As he stared into them, it seemed as if he was frozen in place. He tried to move, but he couldn't! Joey heard Billie Joe making a strange, very soft sound. It was like a growl, but it was so soft it was very hard to hear. Then it rose to a shriek!

"Eeee … orrrr … eeeeeeee! … oeeeeeee!"

The hair rose on Joey's back, and he trembled. When he dared to peek out at Fred, he saw that all of Fred's fur was standing up on end! His tail was all puffed out, and he was crouched as low to the ground as he could get.

Joey was so scared that he deposited a small piece of mouse poop on one of the old boards. He heard Billie Joe's soft padding footsteps as she moved past him. Joey scampered along an escape route his mother had shown him when he was only one-half of a mouse-year old; she had told him never to forget it.

Soon Joey was back in the empty ball of paper, feathers, and fur. He wished some of his brothers and sisters were there to keep him warm.

Adventure Number 3:

Joey Is Caught by Billie Joe

Soon it was summertime, and Joey was three mouse years old. Ignoring his mother's warnings, he spent warm evenings out in the meadows, being much more careful, however. He had two good friends.

One was Fred, who constantly worried about him and was always warning him about Ruby and King, his brother and sister. Fred also warned Joey about his mother, Charlie, who spent most of her time under the porch of the farmhouse—so Joey never went near there.

Joey's other friend was Buck, the big golden retriever. One afternoon, Joey, with a lot of nerve, had crawled right between Buck's paws when he was sleeping in the sunshine on the cement slab in front of the old barn. When Buck woke up, Joey had stood up on his back legs and introduced himself. Buck glanced at him, sort of embarrassed, but finally he just yawned a big yawn and told Joey he knew who he was. He had been smelling him around there ever since the big spring storm. Joey thought that Buck was probably stretching it a bit, but, as usual, he thought better than to say anything.

After that, Buck and Joey had spent many afternoons together by the barn when Buck wanted to take his nap. Buck even growled a bit one time when Ruby ventured too close. But he would let Fred come up and sit down beside them. Buck knew pretty much who liked mice and who didn't.

The other way Joey disobeyed was by ignoring his mother's caution to stay out of the motor home. As he knew he would, he found a space up under the wheel well and squeezed through into the interior. He couldn't believe his eyes! All of the instruments were up front, where there were two large seats looking at the old barn door. Then there was a couch on one side, soft chairs on the other side, and a kitchen, a refrigerator, and even beds! Joey crawled behind a wall in the bathroom and chewed a (very small) hole leading into the insulation space. This allowed him to run around back there where it was dark and the spaces were very small. He even chewed up some toilet paper and took it back into the insulation and made himself a nice nest and pretended he was off on a trip! He found his way, among the wiring, to the front, where he could pretend he was the driver. There, he chewed a (very small) hole where it couldn't be seen, but which allowed him to look down the road. If they were only going down a road! He kept wishing and dreaming.

So, as you can see, Joey was getting adventurous, and at the same time, careless. As he lay safely between Buck's big paws listening to the soft snore of the big dog, he kept wondering what it must be like out in that beautiful meadow that stretched as far as he could see into the afternoon sunlight. He could hear a wren scolding from the roof of her house by the farmhouse, and there, he saw Ruby walking underneath it. He knew that King had wandered off several days earlier and had not been seen since. Lady was in her kennel, and there seemed to be only the hum of the bees working the flowers. At the edge of the woods, he could even see a large doe standing unconcerned in the bright sunlight; surely nothing was going on to be scared about!

At the far end of the meadow, before the old pines, a red-winged blackbird perched on a swaying goldenrod and sang her soft, burring song. A meadowlark seemed to answer from deep in the grass of the meadow, its song falling in sparkling bundles like notes from a lyre. Joey was certain there could be nothing wrong on such a bright day—especially with so many birds singing and watching, to say nothing of the wary mother deer. He had seen, many times, from between Buck's paws how the birds shrieked and warned if they saw a hawk or a fox. There was nothing like that now. So he stuck his nose out and took a good sniff, then ran for the meadow!

When he reached the far end, he was out of breath from running and from excitement. What a beautiful day! And the blackbird was still singing.

Joey was in a bed of wildflowers. A bright orange one had large seed pods at the top and smelled delicious. Joey moved closer to see if he could reach them. The blackbird gave a sharp click and flew off with a noisy flutter. Joey thought he had frightened it, He stood up on his back legs and braced himself with his tail to reach the seed pod.

A thin, wiry black paw snapped from behind a clump of orchard grass, then silver shining claws snapped out, hooking Joey on the front of his chest and snapping him backward. He lit beside the goldenrod stem, rolled over, and ran for a clump of dry grass. The paw snapped again, this time catching his hind end and flipping him end-over-end. It hurt, and he gave a frightened squeak. He struggled to find his feet. As he did, Billie Joe stepped into full view and sat down slowly. Her yellow eyes were sparkling, and she never took them off of Joey. Joey thought of his mother's warnings, which made him feel even more scared.

They sat in the bright sunshine looking at one another. The meadowlark continued to sing, but she had moved higher up into a small elm tree. A red-tailed hawk came into view, circling slowly above them. As its shadow passed quickly over them, Billie Joe glanced up and made a low growl. Joey ran!

13

It was of little use. A lightning-quick paw pinned Joey painfully into the deep grass. He felt Billie Joe's breath, and there was another menacing growl as her teeth fastened behind his neck. He felt himself being lifted into the air, then carried along, swinging back and forth as the cat trotted toward the barn. The razor-sharp fangs painfully pierced the skin of Joey's neck. He was afraid to move or squeak—or even to breathe—for fear she might bite down, hard!

It seemed to Joey that they trotted forever. He had a sickening feeling about what was going to happen. Billie Joe never shared with the other cats. Even when Granny, the farm lady, came with food, Billie Joe would sit off to one side and glare at the other cats, daring them to try to eat first. They never did.

On the cement at the edge of the barn, Billie Joe placed Joey gently on the ground and gave a low, purposeful growl. Charlie was crouched down a safe distance away, watching carefully. Ruby and Fred crept up for a closer look.

Kelly

"Grandma! That's Joey," cried Fred.

Buck heard all of the commotion. He shook his head and got up slowly. He had a sad look on his face when he saw Joey lying between Billie Joe's paws. One thing Buck knew very well: if anyone made the slightest move to take away something from Billie Joe, there would be a flash of claws, whatever it was would be dead, and anyone interfering would have a bloody scratch for their

14

trouble. So Buck eased down onto the warm cement, moving slowly so as not to upset the fierce cat.

Then Kelly ran up. Kelly was the farmer's granddaughter, and she often visited in the summertime. She was a beautiful girl with yellow hair who easily talked with mice (some people do and some don't; Kelly and Jim, the policemen, can, but no one else at the farm could talk with mice).

Kelly saw right away what was going on, and she sat down very slowly beside Buck. She rested her hand on Buck's huge head, as if trying to think about what to do. When Billie Joe saw Kelly watching her closely, she let out a very loud, mean growl. Kelly scratched Buck's head slowly and tried harder to think about what to do. Buck hoped that Kelly didn't forget and scratch that special place behind his ear that always made him kick his back foot, because he knew that would really mess things up!

"Grandma!" Fred said again, "that's my friend, Joey! Don't hurt him!"

Billie Joe stood up quickly, took two quick steps, and swatted Fred four times on the head! The others could hear her claws snagging in his fur and skin. But Fred didn't run away as he usually did; instead, he crouched down and growled back! He laid his ears back along his head (because he knew he was going to get swatted some more). Joey tried to run again, this time for Buck, but Billie Joe turned back effortlessly, swept a paw under Joey's body, and flipped him up in the air. He turned three somersaults and landed with a thud. He couldn't get his breath.

"You're *lazy*, the whole bunch of you," Billie Joe growled at her kittens and Charlie, her daughter. "You've never been hungry a day in your lives! You chase butterflies and eat cat food out of cans. What will you do if these people go away some day? Starve?"

She put a paw on Joey and rolled him over. Buck could feel Kelly's fingers tense in his fur.

"Grandma, let him go," pleaded Fred. He crouched just out of range of those terrible claws. Fred loved his grandma and always stuck up for her when the other kittens made fun of her, even if he was the one she usually swatted. Fred had heard from Charlie that the only time Billie Joe had cried was on that frigid night when they had carried the three kittens all the way through the snow to the farmhouse from across the broad meadows. And after she found the fourth kitten frozen on their last trip back to the road, Fred said, she had never purred again. She had buried that kitten in a snow bank by the road.

But how would Fred know anything? He had been a kitten then himself.

"What's going on here?" It was Granny, the farmer's wife. She was headed for her garden to water her tomato plants. She was wearing a sunbonnet and carrying a pail of water.

"Billie Joe has a mouse," said Kelly. "I'm afraid if I try to take it away, she will kill it."

"Well, that's no problem," replied Granny tartly, and before anyone knew what was happening, that water was out of the pail and landing full force on Billie Joe and Joey.

Billie Joe ran off, shaking herself, and Joey ran straight for the shelter of Buck's forepaws. It was not the last time Joey would hide between the legs of his big friend; it happened again at the prairie-dog town—but I am getting ahead of my story.

Granny was on her way to the garden. Kelly ran for another bucket of water and then reached down and picked up Joey. He was wet and bedraggled and missing some chunks of fur. But he was alive! And the meadowlark was still singing as if nothing had happened.

"That was a close one, fella," Kelly said to Joey, holding him close to her face. She smelled good, thought Joey. Like sunshine and cookies. The thought made Joey think about how hungry he was, and he knew from the smell that Granny had been baking cookies down at the farmhouse. Joey had determined what no one else knew for a fact: the kitchen was not mouse-proof.

Kelly took Joey back into the barn and placed him on the pile of straw where he had been born. Joey pretended that he was asleep so he wouldn't have to crawl inside. He was ashamed to allow his mother to see him all wet and cat-scratched.

Billie Joe ran quickly down the gravel road from the barn. It was actually the same road she had managed to crawl up and down with Charlie that terrible winter when they had been dumped out in the storm.

Billie Joe felt terrible. She glanced back at her grand-kittens, who were starting to play again in front of the barn. She felt very lonely. She looked at Kelly and Buck; by this time, Kelly had Buck lying down, and she was scratching hard in just the right place. The silly dog's feet were kicking about in the air. Kelly would laugh at this and try a new place.

Billie Joe heard the shrill whine of metal. She looked down the gravel road to the machinery shed where Jack, the farmer, was sharpening the blades for the heavy bush-hog mower. There was a shower of sparks with each shriek of the metal. Billie Joe trotted faster. When she reached the shed, she jumped up on the table. Sparks flew all over her.

"Whoa there!" shouted Jack. He stepped back, and the noise stopped, except for the whirring of the wheel. "I swear, Billie Joe," he said, "I've never known a cat who was less afraid of anything than you are!"

He started to move the blade back toward the sharpening wheel, but Billie Joe pushed against him hard, pushing him off balance.

Jack looked down at her. "I see," he said finally. "You want to be picked up. What's going on here? You usually save this sort of thing for the evening."

He placed the large mower blade on the table and turned off the motor. He picked up Billie Joe with both of his hands. As soon as he did this, she twisted around, daring him to drop her. He caught her, but that made him bring her up to his chest. That was what Billie Joe was waiting for. As soon as she felt the rough shirt, she stretched out her long paws and hooked her claws into Jack's collar and pulled herself up to his face. She then rubbed her nose and whiskers into his big bushy mustache. She started to purr so loudly that her whole head sounded like a rattle.

Fred said that Billie Joe liked her family well enough but Jack was the only person in the whole world she really loved. And for once, Fred was exactly right.

Adventure Number 4:

Joey Goes to Disney World!

It didn't seem as long ago as two mouse years after Joey's terrible experience with Billie Joe that he found himself, happy as a lark, riding through the mountains of Tennessee in the freshly washed and shining motor home. He was on his way to Disney World! He was up in his secret place where he could see down the long, curving road ahead—or he could look through a small crack where all of the wires from the television set disappeared. The crack led to a place he had not yet explored. Through the crack, he could see the bald head of the farmer, who was driving, and, if Granny leaned over from her seat across from the farmer, Joey could even see her head, too. They seemed as happy as Joey was, laughing or pointing out the scenery.

Further back, at the breakfast table, sat two additional humans, both children. One was a small boy named Dan who was good at mouse-talk already, probably because he was Kelly's brother (she might have taught him the language). The other was an older girl, very slim, with long dark hair and a beautiful face. Joey had heard from Fred (how did Fred know all of this stuff, anyway?) that the girl's name was Erin and that she was also a granddaughter, she lived in Michigan, and she was learning ballet. Joey wasn't quite certain what ballet was, and he wasn't learning much by listening because Erin didn't speak mouse and was afraid of him. One evening, after the farmer and Granny had gone to bed, Joey had smoothed the fur on his head carefully and cleaned his whiskers before going down to see the two of them, but it didn't help. Erin was still afraid and didn't want to pet him. This made Dan laugh at her, because she was six human-years older than Dan and should have known that Joey would not bite her.

Now, Joey watched through the crack as they played a card game and ate some sugar cookies. Joey's mouth watered when he saw some crumbs falling onto the carpet; they would make a great snack when everyone was asleep, he decided. Everyone, that is, except Buck, who never seemed to sleep much at night because he was so busy worrying about the noises in the camps. As a result, Buck slept all day, usually on the floor between the two seats at the front, where Granny would reach down tickle his ears from time to time. Of course, Joey didn't worry about Buck at night because they were good friends.

The motor home shook as a huge semi truck roared past in the outside lane, and Joey watched as *it* turned on its blinker lights and pulled in front of them. Sometimes the truckers would honk and wave, especially if they had license plates from Ohio. The farmer would honk back. It was fun.

In the campgrounds at night, Joey had learned to be very careful. There were a lot of mice, all locals except for an occasional mouse hitching a ride in a truck or wagon. Joey never met a mouse from another motor home. The local mice acted tough, and they thought that any food left around belonged to them. Also, there were snippy dogs, usually on leashes, and in some camps, a cat snooping around, but fortunately, Joey had not met any who were nearly as skillful as Billie Joe. Despite the risks, Joey often went out for a bit to see how things were. He always made certain that the coast was clear and that he knew the quickest route back to the wheel well on the motor home and safety before he left, though.

On the fourth day of the trip, they were in Florida, and that night they camped in Orlando. The next morning, they set off to explore

Disney World! Joey hitched a ride in Dan's shirt pocket. He considered chewing a (very small) hole so he could see more easily but decided not to do it. Granny was never pleased to find evidence of mice. She had thrown a fit when she'd seen the chewed toilet paper and told the farmer to get some mousetraps, but Joey was relieved that the farmer had never done that.

Joey was confused by the farmer. He was sure that the farmer couldn't speak mouse, but he knew a lot about what was going on.

And Erin was another one. She wasn't doing well at all at learning to understand mouse. Joey wondered if all the words with squeaks at the end made it difficult for her to understand.

Joey peeked out of the shirt pocket—and what a sight he saw! They were walking down a wide street, and a parade was coming toward them, with a loud band

playing. In front, there was a long line of children, dancing, and a lot of animals! Joey found himself jumping up and down in the pocket, but he stopped quickly when he saw Granny staring at Dan, obviously wondering about what was going on in that pocket. So Joey asked Dan to dance around a bit, which he did. When Joey looked out again, Granny was watching the parade.

Then they went into a huge castle where Dan had his photograph taken while getting an autograph from Mickey Mouse, and Erin had several photographs taken, one with Goofy, and one between two squirrels, and probably more. Erin often has the problem of people wanting to take pictures with her. Joey wanted to hop out and get in some of the pictures, but he knew better.

After they had seen all of the sights, they headed for the gate to go to a place called Sea World. On the way, the farmer bought Erin and Dan some cotton candy. It was pink and fluffy. Dan stuffed a little piece into his pocket for Joey, but it wasn't a very good idea. The cotton candy was sticky and it messed up Joey's whiskers. Besides, Joey didn't like the sweet taste.

Joey had a close call at Sea World. There was a huge pool full of dolphins. The dolphins swam around in circles as people threw food to them. Dan had a bag of fish, and before the dolphin show was supposed to begin, he was leaning far over the side of the pool and throwing the little fish to the dolphins. All of a sudden, Joey felt himself slipping out of Dan's pocket—and then he was falling into the pool!

Joey hit with a small splash and started swimming for all he was worth, but his heart sank when he saw that the side of the pool was slick, clear plastic. People saw Joey and started laughing and pointing at him. Then the water parted, and the enormous, slick gray head of a dolphin rose slowly beside Joey. The dolphin's eye was right beside Joey; the eye alone was twice as big as Joey! The huge eye looked him up and down. Joey wondered whether dolphins eat mice.

The dolphin sank slowly out of sight, and Joey swam faster, even though he knew the steep side of the pool made any escape attempt hopeless.

The dolphin's smooth head appeared on the other side of him, *right next to him*, so that the water streaming off of the dolphin's head threatened to swamp Joey. All of the people in the stands were pointing and trying to get others to see what was going on. Joey's heart sank as he saw Erin crying as she watched him struggling in the water.

The dolphin again sank beneath the water. Then Joey felt a funny sensation, as if a big board was coming up under him! He was rising out of the water! He looked down at the slippery gray surface and realized that *he was standing on the dolphin's head!* Joey couldn't believe how far the dolphin was able to rise above the level of the water. A huge blast of air exploded behind Joey, and he almost fell off. He turned, slipping and sliding, to face a huge blow-hole, then, as the dolphin sucked in air, Joey dug in his claws to keep from getting sucked inside. There was a trembling motion, as if a huge motor was churning, and, very slowly, the dolphin moved toward Dan. The dolphin's head was tilted up so much that Joey had to clamber clear up onto the tip of the dolphin's nose. At the very last second, before Joey fell, Dan snatched Joey away!

Everyone clapped and yelled. The dolphin's huge eye stared straight at Joey as the dolphin sank slowly below the clear water. As long as he lived, Joey would never forget the look in that wonderful eye.

Joey shook himself and hopped back into Dan's pocket.

Dan runs back from the dolphin pool holding Joey in his hand!

They camped at Disney World for three days. They had a wonderful time. But on the way home, one thing happened that wasn't pleasant.

Late one night, Joey went for a stroll in a camp in Kentucky. The local mice were, as always, touchy and not very friendly. At the edge of a burned-out campfire, Joey found a tiny piece of toast that had some good flavor in it, sort of like meat. As Joey started to eat it, he heard a snarl behind him. He spun around, and instantly, a large camp mouse was all over him. Joey knew he was in a fight for his life, and he went at it for all he was worth. There was scratching and biting, and fur was flying. The big mouse bit down hard on the tip of Joey's ear, and it really hurt! But Joey fought harder, and he began to feel the other mouse getting tired. Joey kicked him in the stomach twice, and that seemed to do it. The mouse ran off. Joey dragged the tiny piece of toast back to the motor home and hid it in his nest. His ear was bleeding.

The next day, Dan laughed at Joey when he saw it, but then he asked Erin to get the first-aid kit from the bathroom. Erin used a swab to paint some iodine on the tip of the ear. It hurt a lot, but Joey didn't squeak a bit. He knew it was all his own fault. But he also knew that Dan was proud of him because he had stuck up for himself. A little bit of the tip was missing from Joey's ear for the rest of his life, though, and he actually became sort of proud of it. And the girl mice seemed fascinated by it—but that is another story.

Adventure Number 5:

Billie Joe's Story

Sometimes it seems as if even bad things happen for the best. It turned out that way with Billie Joe and Joey, after all. Here's what happened.

Joey could never control himself when it came to going out from the barn at night. He had convinced himself that he was very clever, he had excellent eyes and ears, and, if he took his time and listened before moving, he could go out into the meadow or even into the farmhouse if he felt like it. So he did.

He liked going out at night. First of all, he met a lot of other mice—different mice, such as the meadow mice, who didn't look much like he did. Then there were voles, who were very small and short-tempered. He liked to meet and talk to and see what these others were like. He also liked the quiet. And he liked the big moon that lit everything up, making it almost as bright as daytime.

So Joey roamed—even though his mother had told him many, many times that Joey's father had disappeared on just such a night, last seen kicking in the talons of a huge owl. Joey never knew his father. This had happened a few mouse weeks before Joey was born.

Considering all of this, it cannot really be said that Joey was *surprised* when he heard a low, whispery growl behind him, just as he was finishing a tasty sunflower seed in the moonlight. He knew better than to move, and he hoped desperately that it was some other unlucky mouse or vole that Billie Joe was greeting. Deep down in his little heart, though, Joey knew better. Sure enough, over the tuft of grass appeared that small, nearly black head with those glistening yellow-orange eyes—staring directly at him.

"So, smarty-pants," hissed Billie Joe softly, "here we are again, little mouse, but without that bucket of water to save you!"

In response, Joey did a strange thing. He stood up on his hind legs, pushed the tuft of grass aside, and faced the cat directly. "Billie Joe," he squeaked—he couldn't help squeaking; he was trying to be brave and it wasn't working. "Billie Joe," he began again, "Fred is always sticking up for you. Fred says you're not really mean. Fred says he wouldn't want you to be any different, and you are the one who kept them all alive a long time ago." As he spoke, Joey carefully watched the two soft paws in front of him for any sign of the razor-sharp claws.

"Fred should mind his own business," replied Billie Joe, but her tone had softened somewhat.

"I want to hear about it," demanded Joey.

"Aren't you the one, now," replied Billie Joe sarcastically.

"Well, I'm dead anyway, aren't I?" asked Joey. "What do I have to lose? Were you afraid you were going to die down on that road?"

"That Fred should keep his mouth shut," replied Billie Joe, but her eyes softened, and she seemed far away. She moved softly in the grass. "All right, mouse, I will tell the story. It may help my appetite," she added maliciously.

Joey was smart enough to keep his mouth shut. Billie Joe began to tell the story, almost as if to herself.

It was a bitter-cold winter evening. There was a thick layer of snow on the country roads, and ice was piled at the edges, mixed with salt from the snowplows. It had been a cold, windy week, and every living thing was looking for shelter and warmth.

But shelter and warmth were not to be Billie Joe's lot that night; she and her daughter, Charlie, and Charlie's four newborn kittens had been thrown into a burlap bag by the ugly man who swept up around the back of the grocery store where they had been hiding since the weather had turned cold. He tied up the bag and threw it in the back of an old pickup truck. They had bounced and jolted along the road, with the kittens letting out soft, mewling cries. Billie Joe desperately tore at the burlap. She was certain the man was going to throw them all in the lake at the edge of town. But he kept going.

Billie Joe could hear him laughing and talking to another man in the warm cab, and every so often, they would throw a beer bottle out onto the roadside. The man's driving became uneven, swerving from side to side, and finally, the man slammed on the brakes. They skidded into a mailbox, knocking it sideways, and came to a stop.

"Throw out them cats!" the man shouted. "See, they're bad luck!" Then he laughed, and Billie Joe heard another beer can hiss as he opened it. A short man got out, stepped around, and pulled roughly on the bag. He threw it over his shoulder. Charlie started spitting and scratching inside the bag. The man cursed and threw the bag as far as he could. It landed in a snowdrift.

"Good riddance!" he shouted after them and stumbled back to the truck, which bucked back and forth with the driver swearing at it, until it came loose from the snow and sped off down the road.

Silence fell, and there was no motion in the bag. Then it began to twitch. There was growling, and a tearing sound, and, finally, through a small tear, the small black cat squirmed out onto the snow. Then she started chewing on the hole to make it larger. Charlie finally was able to squeeze out. She stuck her head back inside, trying to find her kittens. The wind was blowing snow across the road, and it was beginning to drift over the burlap bag.

Charlie braced her feet and dragged out a tiny kitten. A second one peeked out of the bag and Billie Joe pulled it out by the neck. The two cats stared at one another in the swirling darkness, and Billie Joe began to trot, with the kitten swinging in her mouth, up the single set of tire tracks that led up a steep hill into the darkness. Charlie followed her.

The wind howled, and the tire tracks seemed to go on forever. The cold pressed relentlessly against them. They finally saw a light in a garage in the back of a large farmhouse, and there they dropped the kittens and stood panting as they looked at the door. It was warmer in the garage, and Charlie lay down, exhausted. Billie Joe looked at Charlie and the kittens nestled under her, then turned and trotted back down the hill.

In the snow bank, she found the burlap bag, now nearly covered. Inside, one kitten mewed weakly. The other was silent. Billie Joe nosed it gently. It was cold. She moved to one side and dug a deep hole in the snow. Slowly she placed the dead kitten at the bottom and scraped snow over it. Then she picked up the last kitten and headed up the steep lane in the blackness, hoping she could make it to the top before it was too late for both of them.

The next morning, the sun rose on a desolate, windswept horizon of snow and ice. The lane ended at a low-roofed farmhouse and garage. Several hundred feet away sagged an old barn with several newer outbuildings behind it.

In the garage, in a pile of rugs, slept a huge golden retriever who seemed as unaware of the coating of snow on his yellow fur as he was of the two cats and three tiny kittens huddled in the far corner, opposite him. The small, dark cat approached the steel bowl beside the dog, hoping to steal some dog food. But the bright bowl was empty! A water bowl beside *it* was frozen solid. The cat sat and waited. The dog snored quietly, then rolled over, spilling off most of the snow. Then he sat up, shook himself, and stared stupidly at the small cat. He wagged his tail for good measure. Then he looked toward the door and gave a soft, "Woof!"

The cat crouched down, for she heard the footsteps as well. Someone was coming to the door!

The door burst open, and a man came out and bent over the dog's bowl. He poured it brimming full with dry food. He was not a large man; he had a bald head with a fringe of gray hair and a large funny–looking, bushy moustache. He had piercing blue eyes, which now glanced over at the cat and then toward the other cat and the kittens. Billie Joe growled a bit in spite of herself.

The farmer knocked out the frozen water bowl and kicked away the chunk of ice. Then he went back into the farmhouse, calling for some milk!

"What for?" a woman's voice asked. "We don't give Buck milk!"

"There's a stray tomcat out there and what looks like a mother and three kittens. The tomcat looks like it's on its last legs. Skinny as a rail. I'm going to feed them."

"Jack, you give those cats milk, and they'll be here forever."

"I don't care, Granny. Nothing is going hungry around my house, especially on the day before Christmas!"

It was a strange sight. The cats watched, fascinated, as the huge bowl was filled with milk. Then Billie Joe ran for it.

"Whoa there," said the farmer as Billie Joe stuck her face deep in the milk and started drinking. "Take it easy, old fellow, we have plenty more, but you'd better slow down, or you'll be sick!"

He watched Charlie creeping up, still afraid. "C'mon partner," he offered. "Looks to me like you need to load up for those kittens."

Billie Joe sat back on her haunches. She did feel a bit sick from all that she had gulped down. She looked at the dog, who continued to wag his tail slowly. Billie Joe looked more carefully at the farmer. He didn't look stupid, but she wondered what kind of farmer would think she was a tomcat. At the moment, though, it didn't seem all that important.

"I think we will call you Billy," said the farmer. Then he shivered and went back into the farmhouse.

During the next two months, Charlie gained weight, and the kittens thrived. But Billie Joe remained thin and tough. She moved them into the barn, and they took over the old horse trough. All of them liked Buck, and he usually stayed in the barn with them, almost as if he was protecting them. Sagebrush, the dog who belonged to Jim, the policeman who lived at the bottom of the hill, came tearing up one early spring day. Billie Joe settled that matter once and for all by facing him down; Billie Joe threw in a few lightning swats of her claws for good measure.

The cats all acquired names for the first time. The farmer's grandchildren, when they visited, were allowed to name the kittens, whom they called Ruby, King, and Fred—properly, as it turned out; Granny named Charlie, even though she was female. The farmer finally figured out Billie Joe was a female as well, so he called her Billie Joe. He seemed to be a little embarrassed.

Jack, the farmer, liked to say that he had never seen a cat as fast as Billie Joe or one who was so unafraid of anything that lived. But that was not necessarily enough, as she found out.

One night, when Billie Joe was out hunting in the moonlight, she barely escaped the rush of a hunting coyote. Billie Joe knew they were around. She had heard them yip in the night in the moonlight, but the attack took her by surprise. No swatting on her part would have helped a bit. If there had not been a tall pine tree beside her, that would have been the end of Billie Joe.

Perhaps that is why Billie Joe now looked down at the small mouse and asked, "What did you say your name was, little fellow?"

"I'm Joey ... Billie Joe," he replied. His voice didn't squeak this time. He really wasn't very scared anymore.

"Well, Mr. Joey," you need to be more careful. There are things out here that are too big for you." And without another word, the small, black, sinewy cat silently slipped away into the deeper grass of the meadow.

Adventure Number 6:

Joey Goes for a Ride in a Police Cruiser

In Joey's fifteenth mouse year, he made friends with Jim, the policeman. It was summertime, and Joey was bored with some of his mouse friends; perhaps he was just plain bored. Anyway, he had been talking to Fred about Jim, the policeman, who lived down at the bottom of the hill with his wife, Lisa, in a brand-new house that was supposed to be mouse-proof. Fred claimed that Jim could to talk to mice, but he admitted that very few grown-up humans did. Fred said that Jim trained big dogs for the policemen and that was how he talked to mice. When Joey asked Fred what that had to do with talking with mice, Fred got mad and went off in a huff.

Joey thought about all of this carefully. He knew about Sagebrush, Jim's large farm dog, who looked more like a coyote than a dog. Sagebrush lived in a big pen down the hill, but Jim let him out when he went to work so Sagebrush could protect Lisa. Only sometimes, especially when he first got out, Sagebrush would come tearing up the hill at breakneck speed and chase anything that moved! All the mice and cats hated

Lady is trying to make friends with Sagebrush

33

Sagebrush, and the woodchucks and squirrels were especially angry because nothing spoiled a nice summer day more some big crazy dog tearing through the meadow just when they had started to chew on some tasty seeds.

Joey also knew that he had to be very careful about Lisa. He had heard that she kept a very neat house. The few times she had come up to the farmhouse, she had been neat and clean and all dressed up. She just didn't *look* like she liked mice—and he was sure she couldn't talk mouse.

One night, Joey left the old barn after dark. The summer evening had been very long, and he had waited until he was sure humans couldn't see very much. Of course he (and the cats and everything else) could see just fine. He stood outside and listened carefully. All he heard was a barred owl hooting back in the woods. He saw Buck watching him from the concrete in front of the barn. Buck was slowly wagging his tail. Buck never seemed to get tired of wagging his tail. It made a soft swishing noise as it brushed over some old leaves.

"Going somewhere, little fellow?" he asked.

"I'm going down to see Jim," announced Joey. A soft evening breeze was blowing across the cement. It was damp with dew and smelled wonderful.

"Jim doesn't get home this early," replied Buck. "Not until eleven. He works the afternoon shift." Buck felt like he was sort of a policeman, like Jim, and he was proud to know the details.

"It will take a long time for me to get down there," answered Joey. "I'm going to stop to see a little field mouse I met last week."

Buck rolled his eyes but said nothing.

It was much later when Joey slipped past Sagebrush's pen (she was snoring loudly, no doubt worn out from chasing everything all day), and headed down to the edge of the chimney at the house. Joey heard Jim's pickup truck on the gravel as he was finishing the (very small) hole he had chewed where he had found a small crack between the chimney and the side of the house. It took only several minutes

The policeman

more for him to find his way through the insulation and a loose piece of duct tape at the edge of a heating duct. After running along the duct, he squeezed through a dented place where the duct was fastened to a heating register, and he was out in the laundry room! He ran down the stairs to a lower level, where he heard Jim moving around.

As he scampered through the doorway, Jim was placing his service revolver on a table and had turned toward to a gun rack to get a cleaning rag and a can of oil. When Jim turned around, Joey was standing on the table beside Jim's gun. Jim acted as if he didn't see him. He sat down on a stool and squirted oil on a small round rag. Joey's nose twitched. He liked the way the oil smelled.

Joey stood up on his back legs. "I'm Joey," he announced.

Jim looked at him sharply. Jim had a thin face and high cheekbones. His eyes were bright blue, and his hair and eyebrows were light brown. With his uniform and badge and all, he reminded Joey of a character in a Clint Eastwood movie he had watched once with Kelly up at the farmhouse.

"Buck tells me you're a wise guy," said Jim. That sounded tough, but Joey knew from his voice that he was kidding. Jim started to take the gun apart. He put the pieces on the table after he cleaned each one and rubbed it with the oily rag.

Joey looked around the room. It was full of strange stuff! There was a thick black vest with "Swat Team" printed on the back and an orange raincoat hanging beside it. Then there was a gun cabinet where rifles and shotguns and several pistols gleamed in the soft light. One shotgun had a laser light strapped under the barrel. "Wow!" said Joey, mostly to himself.

Jim snapped the cylinder back into his revolver and spun it. It made a soft clicking sound. "Since you're such a wise guy," continued Jim, "I assume you're not afraid of kids, are you?"

"Of course not. Kelly and I are good friends. And I'm not afraid of Erin, even if she doesn't like me," answered Joey.

"I mean kids you don't know. Kids that are just getting out of school, and the only mouse they have ever seen is one with a broken neck." said Jim.

"Well ..." Joey wasn't too sure about that.

"I tell you what, Mr. Wise Guy. I will make up a little cardboard house out of a small box and put it on the dashboard of my cruiser. And when I park to watch the kids coming out of school tomorrow, you can come out of the box. If they stop by, you can run back into the house if you're scared and all."

"I didn't say I was scared. I'm not scared of anything."

Jim laughed. "Then I'll call you tough guy instead of wise guy. We will see. Now get out of here, and don't make any messes anywhere."

It seemed to Joey that the next day would never come, but of course it did. Never had mouse time gone so slowly. Finally, they were in Jim's pickup truck, headed for Bellefontaine. Jim was wearing yellow sunglasses against the afternoon sun slanting across the dashboard, where Joey rode in a small cardboard box that Jim had painted to look like a jail. *It was hot in there! And just one small door! What if some kid picked up the box and started shaking it?* Joey wasn't too sure about all of this.

Sure enough, the kids streaming out of the school spotted Jim sitting up the street in his cruiser. Many just waved as they ran past and crossed the street at the stoplight at the corner, but several came over to see what was going on. Jim teased them that he was going to arrest them if they didn't hurry home and do their homework. As soon as they saw the box they wanted to know what was going on.

"I have a prisoner in there," said Jim. They all laughed at him.

"Show me," said one kid. He looked pretty bright. The other kids took up the challenge.

"He's too dangerous," said Jim. He might get away, and I'd have to go capture him all over."

"Pooh!" said a bigger kid standing in the back.

"Yeah," said a voice from just below the edge of the cruiser window, where a small boy barely poked his nose up to the sill, his fingers clutching the edge of the window. "Show us!" he demanded, but he backed away when Jim leaned over and looked down at him.

"Never argue with a cop about his prisoners." said Jim. "This prisoner's name is Joey. He has an alias: the Motor-Home Mouse!"

"Show us! Show us!" they shouted.

Jim put his fingers in his mouth and blew a screeching whistle. Joey hated it when Jim did that, even from far away. As it was, with him all cooped up in that box, the sound nearly deafened him. Besides, Jim did that to call Sagebrush; even the squirrels and woodchucks hated the whistle. Joey stuck his nose out of the door.

"Look! A mouse! A real mouse!" shouted the little boy, who had grabbed onto the edge of the window and pulled himself up so he could see the action.

Joey crawled out onto the dashboard and stood up on his back legs. Excited faces filled the open window.

"He was arrested for not being in school." said Jim.

"Mice don't go to school!" they shouted. Joey decided to go back into the box.

"Let me take him home!" demanded the tall boy in the back. "I'll feed him to my cat."

Joey felt the box lifting off of the dashboard. He dropped a small piece of mouse poop on the cardboard in spite of himself.

Then Jim laughed and put the box back down. "Go on, kids," he said. "I've got to take my prisoner in and book him." He started the engine and inched slowly away from the curb. The kids were shouting and laughing after him as he pulled away.

The trouble didn't start until after they had eaten dinner. Jim ordered a cheeseburger at Wendy's and shoved a small piece of the bun into the jail. It had just the right amount of ketchup on it, and Joey ate every bite. Then they started cruising.

An hour later, as they were stopped at a four-way stop-sign, a large Cadillac swerved through the intersection, made a screeching right turn, and sped off down the street. Jim switched on his flashing roof lights and pressed down on the accelerator, and they shot after the Cadillac. The jail was sliding back and forth on the dashboard, so Joey jumped out of it and dug in his claws to hold on. He had to dodge the box as it slid back when they turned another sharp corner. He was sorry he had eaten so much supper.

When they caught up with the speeding car, Jim turned on his siren briefly and then snapped it off. The Cadillac slowed and pulled over to the curb. Jim called in the license number to the dispatcher at the police station. The radio crackled back at them after a brief pause. When the dispatcher's voice came back on it held a note of warning. "Jim," he said slowly, "do you know that's Judge Rutherford's car?"

"I know, Steve. It's the judge's wife doing the driving."

"Jim … I've got to let the chief know about this." Steve sounded miserable.

"Steve, you do what you have to do, and I will do the same." The radio hummed but was silent.

Jim stepped out of the cruiser, the flashing red and blue lights making streaks across his chest. Joey crawled down to the corner by the window so he could listen.

"Good evening," said Jim as he walked up to the window.

"Did I do something wrong, officer?" She was a pretty woman, dressed in a sun suit. She had a dark tan and seemed unconcerned about whether she had done anything wrong.

"May I see your license, please?" asked Jim.

The woman started to fumble in her purse. Even back in the cruiser Joey could smell alcohol—but then mice can smell almost anything, no matter how far away. She stopped fumbling and threw the purse onto the seat beside her. "Look, she said, "let's not play games. I'm Ellen Rutherford … Judge Rutherford's wife." Her voice was rising, and she was talking louder. "I will ask him to check with you in the morning. I'm certain we can get this all straightened out. I've been playing golf … and stayed over a bit … and I need to get home. My family may be worried."

Jim ignored the remarks. "I need to see your license," he repeated.

The woman glared at Jim. She placed her hand on the keys in the ignition. "What would you do if I just drove off?" she asked nastily.

Jim looked at her steadily. Joey knew exactly how it felt to have Jim look at you like that. "If you try to drive off, I will pull you out of the car, put handcuffs on you, and take you down to the station and book you."

Ellen Rutherford made sort of a growling noise, sort of like the one Billie Joe makes just before she swats one of her grandchildren three or four times. She picked up the purse and started fumbling again. A shadow went past Joey. It was a large policeman with a lot of bars on the shoulder of his uniform. He stepped up to the window of the Cadillac, glancing at Jim and then inside the car.

"Evening, Ellen," he said. Joey didn't like the way he sounded.

"Oh, hello, *Chief,*" she replied, glancing over at Jim and smirking.

"What's the trouble?" asked the chief.

"Let her tell you," said Jim. He walked back to the cruiser, pulled out a clipboard, and started to fill out a ticket.

The chief walked back behind him. "She says you threatened to haul her out of the cruiser and book her downtown," the chief said accusingly.

"Like I said, Chief, let her tell it."

"You writing a ticket?"

"She was doing sixty down Hayes Avenue."

"You clocked it?"

"Yep."

"What about the drinking?"

"I can't prove anything. If someone else takes her home, I'm not trying to prove anything."

"I'll drive her home."

"Good for you."

"You don't make many friends around here, you know, Jim."

"I don't get paid to make friends, Chief." He tore off the ticket and handed it to the chief and crawled back into the cruiser. As he passed the Cadillac, Ellen Rutherford waved at him and then laughed.

They started cruising again. Jim seemed to be thinking private thoughts, and Joey knew better than to say anything. After an hour of gliding slowly along the darkened streets, they were at the far end of town when Jim suddenly gunned the engine. The cruiser twisted into a huge parking lot and screeched to a stop at the corner of a darkened store. Only then did Joey see a man with a knife crouching in the shadow of the building.

"Hey, Pierce!" shouted Jim. "Stop that! Put that bale of straw back on that stack!"

"Aw, Jim," the man said slowly. "I ain't hurtin' nuthin'. I wuz just gettin' this to make a little dry bed over around the corner there." He nodded toward a clump of trees.

"Put it back!" Jim insisted.

The man was huge. He was wearing a tattered undershirt and dirty denim pants. He was barefoot. He threw the bale of straw back onto the pile in front of the building. He looked like he could have thrown it over the building if he had felt like it.

"And put away that pig-sticker before somebody starts screaming you're trying to rob them," demanded Jim. "Then I'd have to shoot you."

Pierce smiled slowly at Jim and folded his long pocket knife and slipped it into his pocket. "I know you'd never shoot me, Jim," he replied. "'Cause you and me, we're friends. Anyway, I was just going to cut the binder twine on that bale. You know, make up my bed."

"Get in here, Pierce," said Jim. The big man walked around the cruiser and slid into the front seat. He smelled so bad that Joey's nose wouldn't stop twitching. It even made Joey dizzy. Mice smell so well that a strong bad smell affects them.

"We're going downtown to the soup kitchen, Pierce. They might even find a bed for you." Now Joey smelled more alcohol. *Does everybody in this town smell like that?* he wondered.

Pierce saw Joey looking at him from the door on the box. "Hey, Jim," he said. "You got a pet mouse! I ain't seen one of them since some guy had one in Korea. Ain't he something!" He reached unsteadily for the box.

"You can't have him, Pierce," said Jim. "That's my deputy. He can fight like a tiger!"

"Aw, Jim," said Pierce, smiling. "You're kidding me again about me pulling them guys off of you when they jumped you in that bar, ain't you."

Jim smiled over at him. "Might have been different without you, Pierce."

They pulled up in front of a storefront without a sign. Pierce ambled toward the door. Inside, several men were serving themselves at a long table. A tired waitress in the back waved to Jim as they pulled away.

Joey didn't say a word all the way home. He stayed in the small box. At the lane to the farm, Jim drove past his house and up the long road to the farmhouse and pulled up to the old barn. Buck came out, wagging his tail. Jim touched the tip of his finger to the brim of his hat when he saw Buck. Buck wagged his tail even faster. It was sort of like a salute between two professionals.

"Good night, partner," said Jim to Joey quietly. "Go tell Buck how much fun it is to be a cop."

Adventure Number 7:

Joey Visits a Prairie Dog Town

Joey, along with Erin, the granddaughter from Michigan, visited a prairie dog town. First they visited Deadwood, in the prairie state of South Dakota. That was not all bad, although in Deadwood, Joey did not leave the motor home. It was a rough mining town in the Old West, and it had never quite lost that rough character. There were a lot of motorcycles around, and who knows what kind of tough stray cats, so Joey had snuggled into his nest beside the warm thing that converted the current from the campground to something that the motor home could use. (At least, that was what the farmer said it did. All Joey knew was that it hummed all of the time when they were in camp, and it was always warm.)

Joey was enjoying the nice smell of straw. He had chewed a hole (very small) in a new straw hat that Granny had purchased at a store. They had been up on the mountainside where there were presidents' faces carved in stone, all of them looking wonderfully grave. Granny had purchased the hat because it was a hot day, and the sun was very bright, but then she seemed to have forgotten about it in the closet.

Once the hole was in the hat, Joey knew that it didn't look very nice. He had decided to go ahead and chew up the brim, too. He made a new lining for his nest with the straw. He felt guilty about it, but after all, he was a mouse. Mice do things like that.

After Deadwood, they drove all afternoon through some rough country called badlands. The drive was boring because the farmer was telling stories about his grandfather in Deadwood, and the stories went on and on until Joey fell asleep in the back of the television set. If anyone had turned the set on, they would have had fried mouse.

Joey did see several antelope out of his peephole when the farmer pointed to them, far away, up on a hill covered with sagebrush. The antelope stood around in small groups, but if they thought anyone was watching, they would run away like the wind!

Joey had a good supper in camp—he had found an ice-cream cone with some melted strawberry ice cream at the very bottom, and, perhaps because he was so stuffed with all of that, he dreamed of the mountain with all of the presidents—Washington, Jefferson, Lincoln, and Roosevelt—with the sun shining on them like they were still alive. He dreamed that he crawled out on Jefferson's nose and stood up on his hind legs for all of the tourists to see.

They found the prairie dog town as they were about to leave South Dakota, and Erin begged the farmer to stop so she could see

Erin

the prairie dogs. So they pulled into the large state park that included the prairie-dog town. The park protected the prairie dogs from all of the humans who like to shoot them for fun—fun not for the prairie dogs, fun for the humans who like to shoot them.

Joey liked Erin, even if she didn't like him very much. He liked the Irish freckles all over her nose, and he liked her for a

45

lot of other reasons as well. She was just neat, that was all there was to it. Also, she would ask Joey about stuff rather than asking someone else, even though she didn't speak mouse very well.

"Why do they live in towns?" she asked Joey. She assumed that he knew everything about rodents.

"They're very social," explained Joey, not able to think of anything better at the moment.

"Big towns?" asked Erin.

"Very big," said Joey, "Even a mile across." He wasn't positive about that, but it sounded good.

"Gee!" exclaimed Erin. "Let's go!"

The prairie dog town was big, but not nearly a mile across. The farmer parked the motor home in a huge parking lot where a ranger was busy painting the fence. Inside the fence, as far as they could see, were mounds of dirt, and on top of most of them sat prairie dogs! The prairie dogs kept looking around. If they saw something they didn't like, they would give two short barks and dive into their holes

Erin slipped around to the wheel well by the back tire, where Joey met her and hopped into the pocket of her shirt. He was careful not to scratch her through the shirt because anything like that gave Erin the heebie-jeebies, and Joey didn't want to miss the ride.

They walked along the edge of the park, through the long grass. The ranger smiled at Erin as she passed. The ranger's big dog, an Irish setter, looked at Erin and wagged his tail, then sniffed, looking puzzled as he caught a whiff of Joey. All dogs like Erin.

They stopped at the edge of the prairie dog town, where there was a huge sign that said "No Pets."

The sun was very bright. It was hot and dusty. The first mound of earth was about ten feet from them, with a big hole beside it. There was no prairie dog on it. Twenty feet away, the nearest prairie dog watched them carefully.

46

"Well," said Joey, "in for a penny, in for a dollar!" And without another word he jumped out of Erin's shirt and darted down the nearest hole! The nearby sentinel gave two sharp barks and dived into its hole, and all over the town, the prairie dogs barked and dived underground!

It was still hot and dusty as Joey ran down the first several feet of the burrow, but then it turned cool and just barely damp. Joey realized why the prairie dogs lived like this, down in the soft, clean earth. He ran by many side tunnels, and here and there, he could see what looked like living quarters filled with families; in other places, he saw small rooms filled with grass and grain. A long way before him, down the tunnel, Joey could see a large prairie dog hurrying toward him.

"You there!" the prairie dog shouted, but it came out sort of huffy because he was fat and out of breath. He tried to stand up as he reached Joey, but the tunnel was too low, and he hit his head. A shower of dirt ran down the fur on his neck. "You there!" he repeated, even though he was right in front of Joey. "What are you doing in here?"

Joey did his best to look meek, but he was not very good at it because he was not meek at all. "Well, sir," he said in his best fake-meek voice, "I'm from Ohio and I came down to find out about prairie dogs."

The prairie dog turned around and shouted back down the tunnel. "It's all right! It's just another dumb tourist. Tell the sentinels to get back up top!" He sounded very important. Then he turned back to Joey. His tone was polite, but it sounded like he was bored from repeating the same thing over and over. "In the first place," he said, yawning slightly as he finished, "we're not dogs; we're rodents."

"I know that," replied Joey. "I know all that stuff. I'm a rodent, too, you know."

"We are black-tailed prairie dogs," continued the guide, as if he had not heard anything Joey had said, "as opposed to white-tailed prairie dogs. *Cynomys ludovicianus,*" he explained further. He was really wound up.

"*Cynomys ludovicianus!*" he shouted. "Once, we covered the western prairies! We were important turners of the soil! We brought up clay and let air and water in! Buffaloes wallowed in our towns!" He stopped suddenly as a thought hit him.

"P … pardon me," interrupted Joey, "could I look around a little bit? I really don't have much time."

The elder prairie dog looked insulted. "None of you tourists ever do," he replied stiffly. "Go ahead and look around. I can't stop you. Everyone else helps themselves; why not you? There were two marmots down here last week looking around; why not you?" With that, he turned and went off down the tunnel until he was lost in the darkness.

Now the tunnel seemed very empty and spooky. Joey ran along, turning here and there until suddenly he was not certain he knew his way back! Just as he was starting to worry, he heard mice talking. At first, he couldn't be sure. The voices were very soft, but as he followed them, he became sure it was mice talking, although they had a strange accent. Finally, he came to a small hole. Peeking inside, he saw a large family of strange-looking mice.

"*Ahem!*" he said loudly. They all turned to stare at him. "Do you have a doorway?" he asked. "Surely you don't stay in there all the time."

One of the mice, obviously the mother, said rather tartly, "We block up the entrance every afternoon. Otherwise, we might very well be supper for the black-footed ferret!"

"I've never heard of such a thing before," replied Joey. But then, he had never heard of a black-footed ferret either.

"All plains pocket mice block up their entrances during the day," the mother answered. "We have been doing that for years."

"What kind of mouse is that?" asked Joey.

"Plains pocket mouse," said the mother. *"Perognathus flavescens!"*

"Oh," said Joey.

"Actually, we are just one of a group living here. There are also silky pocket mice, apache pocket mice, and occasionally a hispid pocket mouse, but they are very large and stupid. The black-footed ferret gets them easily—if the burrowing owls, coyotes, or rattlesnakes don't get them first!" She shuddered when she mentioned the rattlesnakes.

"Excuse me," said Joey politely, for he was beginning to feel strange. "Could you tell me which of these paths go back to the parking lot?"

"You tourists never know anything," snapped the mother, but she moved up close to the hole to point down one of the paths. But her eyes widened at what she saw!

"Children!" she squeaked, "Run, run! Out the back hole quickly! I see the ferret!" She quickly disappeared from the hole, and there were scrambling sounds everywhere. Joey turned to look, and what he saw almost froze the blood in his veins. Far down the dark tunnel was a fierce face with a black mask across it—exactly like a bandit's mask. The rest of the animal's fur was milky white, and the fast-moving legs were dusky. It had spotted Joey in the dim light and was running toward him. Joey could hear the barks of the sentinels everywhere echoing down the tunnels. He turned and ran for his life up the tunnel the pocket mouse had indicated.

As he ran, he knew that the ferret was gaining on him. Then he heard a sound he could not believe. It was a very faint *Harroof!* But he recognized it! He ran for all he was worth. That sound had to be old Buck!

As he scrambled, he could hear only the scratchy sound of his feet, but, although the ferret made no sound, he knew it was closer. He took a chance and glanced backward. There it was, gaining rapidly, running with a silvery, silent quickness. Every motion spelled doom!

But now there was a nearer, louder noise!

"Grrrough! Grrrough! Ruff!" What a loud noise. It was old Buck!

The barking was stirring leaves and dirt, and the light was much brighter. The ferret hesitated a second before it took a final leap. Joey could feel its breath.

Then there was an incredibly loud *"Woof!"* It sounded almost like thunder! It knocked Joey back for a second, then he rolled quickly and burst into the sunlight—right at Buck's feet! Just then, Buck opened his mouth for another bellow. Joey could see clear down Buck's pink throat, and he ducked before the blast came out or it would have blown him back down the tunnel. He could see Buck's cheeks blow out with the noise, and afterward, Buck's lips were dripping saliva and spray flew everywhere.

The ferret stuck his nose out of the hole and hissed in rage. Joey never knew Buck could be so quick. Like a flash, he snapped at the nose, barely missing as it disappeared. Buck kept barking. Joey could hear the ferret hissing as the sound faded down the tunnel.

Finally Buck stared down at Joey.

Joey looked up at Buck. Buck's two huge front legs rose above him like furry telephone poles. Buck's mouth was still dripping. Joey started to say something, but he never got the chance.

"Look here, little fellow," snapped Buck (who was still very angry). "I do my best to see that everyone in my extended family is safe!" He stopped and panted several times. This worried Joey, as he knew that Buck was many, many mouse years old, and such things were hard on him. "But I can't be *everywhere!*" he complained. "You have *no business out here!* Let alone down some hole where I can't help you. If the ranger's setter hadn't warned me that he smelled you go by and watched you dive in there, you would have been done-for!" Buck was panting and very much out of breath.

"Buck!" It was the farmer calling. He was angry because Buck was out of the motor home, which was against park rules, and he did not want the ranger to get angry. Buck turned and trotted toward the motor home. Erin was standing in front of it. She looked worried.

Joey ran as fast as he could through the tall grass. He knew that the farmer was in a hurry, and he was afraid that he might not make it. The big setter glanced at him as he went past and wagged his tail. He seemed amused. Joey later heard the farmer telling Granny that the ranger loved those black-footed ferrets and that they are rare because the prairie dog towns are disappearing.

Joey managed to crawl up through the wheel well just as the farmer started the motor. He heard Erin crying. He crept along, through the insulation, looking for a spot where he could show himself to her or give a squeak if he couldn't show himself.

"What's wrong with her?" he heard the farmer ask as the motor home started to roll.

"Something about a mouse," answered Granny. "Sometimes, I don't understand that girl."

Erin found Buck and Joey back by the beds. They were on the highway headed for home. She put her arms around Buck's huge neck and hugged him. "Thank you for saving Joey," she said quietly, even though, with the noise of the motor, no one but Joey or Buck could possibly hear her.

"I was just doing my job," replied Buck. Buck was trying to act modest, but Joey knew that Buck was very proud of what he had done. Joey was careful not to hop over onto Erin—even though he wanted to. He was between Buck's two paws, and he stayed there because he knew Erin was touchy about mice. He wished Erin would hug him the way she did Buck. He loved Erin with the freckled nose and shining eyes.

Adventure Number 8:

Miss Sara Kirby's Visit

Joey was fourteen mouse years old when Miss Sara Kirby came to the farm to visit. He never forgot that visit because it was the only time he ever used a backward-looking spyglass.

It all started on a wonderful, warm, sunny day when Joey was loafing with three cats on the warm cement in front of the old barn where the motor home was parked. The cats were Charlie, Ruby, and Joey's special friend, Fred. Both were nearly full-grown. The other kitten, King, had wandered off one day and had never been seen since; Charlie was pretty certain that a coyote had caught him.

They all were keeping an eye out for Billie Joe because they never knew what sort of mood the old black grandmother cat might be in. She hated seeing them loafing in the sun, and for all Joey knew, she might blame him in some way and change her mind and eat him. None of them were taking any chances. If Billie Joe swatted someone, it was with her claws out. There was nothing about a love tap in her swats, and she never seemed to swat a kitten just once. She could deliver four swats in the time it took most cats to get off just one.

But, according to Fred, who seemed to have all the latest news, Billie Joe was down at the Jim's house, hunting around in the trees for chipmunks. Of course, the chipmunks had been warned by a series of whistles from nest to nest, all the way down the hill, but there was always some dumb chipmunk who was too busy to pay attention. Or so it seemed.

So Joey was sitting on a pile of straw, nibbling on a piece of corn he had picked off of a pile where the farmer had spilled it as he made a sharp turn around the barn with his wagon. The mice had quickly cleaned most of it up and stored it away, but Joey was enjoying one of the left-over grains. Joey started on the piece of corn at the tip and chewed slowly, enjoying it as if it were an ice-cream cone, and he was looking forward to the best part, the kernel, which was a brighter-orange piece near the bottom.

"Miss Sara Kirby is coming," announced Fred. Fred is Charlie's second kitten, and he hangs out around the farmhouse and listens to all of the gossip. He stays around even after the pets have all been fed because he likes to know it all. And he usually does.

"Who is Miss Sara Kirby?" asked Joey, and he chewed more slowly.

"She's a girl who lives up in Charlevoix, which is in Michigan," said Fred importantly. He had heard that, but he had no idea what it meant.

"Big deal," said Joey.

"Her father is really fat," continued Fred, "but Miss Sara is not. Miss Sara Kirby is very pretty ... they say."

Joey started to show a bit more interest. "Why is she coming?"

"With her mother," replied Fred. Fred never made any sense when he ran out of information. "She likes cats," he continued lamely. Fred fell silent. That was all he had heard before Granny had shooed him awayafter she stumbled over him as she came out onto the front porch.

Ruby stood up and stretched in the warm sunshine. "If she likes cats," she said, "I hope Granny lets her feed us. When she lets Kelly feed us, we get a whole lot of food!"

So it was no surprise when, later that afternoon, the farmer arrived from West Liberty with Miss Sara Kirby and her mother in the old red truck. The truck rattled a lot and had a hole in the floorboards, and Miss Sara looked a little dusty as she stepped down from it. The cats gathered around to inspect her, along with Buck. Joey was hiding in a secret place at the edge of the porch.

Miss Sara Kirby was twelve human-years old, tall, blonde, and very beautiful. Her hair was long, and it was fastened, with a silver clasp, behind her neck, which was a bit sweaty. She reminded Buck of Kelly, so he didn't have the heart to woof at her and scare her as a sort of joke—something he tried on most girls. He just wagged his tail at her.

The farmer brought out the golf cart for Sara to ride around the farm, and the rest of the humans went inside. Buck clambered up on the seat beside her, and, at the last minute, Joey hitched a ride by hopping on the back and hanging on to the underside of the armrest on Buck's side. It was a mistake. Miss Sara Kirby took off like a rocket, and Joey could barely hang on. At every bump, he hit his head on the underside of the armrest. Buck was having a terrible time as well, but Miss Sara put one arm around his neck to hold him on the cart, and she drove with one hand. She just about threw all three of them off into a deep rut down by the lake. When they passed the barn for the third time, Joey hopped off, rolled end-over-end, and ran into the barn rubbing his head. After a bit, Buck came back slowly and sank down outside, giving off a long sigh. Sara had gone inside for a soda. Buck was ready to sneak out into the meadow if she came after him again.

The very next day, the big adventure happened, the adventure that none of the adults ever knew about. The three cats talked Joey into going all the way to the Indian camp, a place he knew about but where he and his friends never went because it was so spooky. Joey had found the camp one day while digging for seeds. He had found a tiny piece of ruby red glass at the camp, a place he had no business being since it was so far from the barn and over several steep ravines covered with huge trees that shut out all of the sunlight. But Joey was always where he wasn't supposed to be. *Anyway*, the glass was about as large as a teardrop and had a small gold handle. It was very old but not spoiled at all by time. A very old (several hundred mouse years

old) lady mouse whom Joey had befriended by giving her extra food in the winter told Joey, when he showed it to her, that it was a magical piece of glass, probably lost by some gypsies or even an Indian medicine man. She called it a backward spyglass, but she wouldn't look through it. She told Joey that he never should look through it, that only young *innocent* girls should look through such a thing. Joey tried it anyway, as soon as he was out of her sight, but absolutely nothing happened. He decided that he should take it on their adventure, and if nothing happened with it, he was going to throw it away.

They went south from the farmhouse and were soon in the deep forest. The cats were very cautious. Several deer stared as the group filed silently past them. In a very dark glen, they surprised a hen turkey on her nest, and she rushed off with a great flapping of wings that scared the wits out of Miss Sara Kirby. She wanted to go back, but Joey talked to the cats at length and they convinced Miss Sara Kirby to continue. Miss Kirby didn't talk mouse, which was a nuisance.

They arrived at the Indian camp about four o'clock in the afternoon. In the dense woods, it was cool and dim, and it was very quiet except for the humming of the summer insects. Far in the distance, several crows cawed loudly.

The floor of the forest was covered with hickory nuts, and at the edge of the camp, there were huge beech trees standing—exactly

as they had stood when the Indians sheltered among them over a hundred human-years ago. At the very center of the clearing, there was an ancient fire pit. At the edge, there was a stream that widened into a large pool, gathering the cold, clear water before it ran off down Indian Run toward the Mad River.

Joey stepped out and reached up toward Sara, reaching up as far as he could. He held the ruby glass out to her. She bent down to see what the tiny mouse was showing her. Curious, she took the glass, turned it back and forth, and finally held it up to her eye and looked at the campsite.

As she stared, Sara could not believe her eyes! She looked down at herself. She was wearing a leather shirt, long leggings, a tippet (a garment like a large scarf that is worn thrown over the shoulders), and moccasins! The shirt was of the softest elk hide with fringes running along the sleeves, as were the leggings. The tippet had a collar of otter skin, with a tail at one end and the eyes and jaws at the other! Hanging down her back from the otter skin were rows of ermine tails covering her shoulders. Her long, braided hair was jet black with eagle feathers woven into it, and the moccasins were covered with tiny beads. And Sara's skin was as dark brown as that of the other humans she saw moving toward her!

Her vision widened. There were dark-skinned people moving about the camp, all with long, straight, black hair. The women were dark-eyed, their skin very smooth, and they motioned to Sara as they moved about, but she couldn't understand what they meant.

An old man approached her deferentially. He seemed at a loss to speak. Sara was more than a little frightened, although she could still see Joey standing up on his back legs beside her right foot, and he seemed to be enjoying himself immensely. "M … my name is … Sara," she stammered at the old man.

He was wrinkled and as dark brown as coffee. He tried to say "Sara," but then he said a very long name in his language. Sara learned finally that her name to them was "Tall Woman Running," and she was never called anything else when she was with them. She learned that there was great excitement in the village because the warriors had just captured a famous white man, Mr. Simon Kenton, and all of the children had been sent to cut blackberry switches because Kenton was going to be forced to run the gauntlet.

They formed a long line that stretched from the top of the sparkling stream down to the pond—the children laughing and practicing with their switches, the old squaws brandishing some heavier clubs, and behind them, a line of warriors watching the captive with hooded eyes that glinted dangerously.

Kenton was dressed in a leather shirt and leather stockings, which were soaked with sweat because he had run for miles behind the horse of Barking Dog. Barking Dog, a warrior, was the head of the band that had surprised Kenton in the valley and captured him.

Kenton was powerfully built but with a slight paunch and a shiny bald head. He was brought over and thrown on the ground before the old man and Tall Woman Running. When the man looked up at Sara, his face was covered with grime from the fire pit.

"Uncle Ned!" exclaimed Sara, putting her hand to her mouth in surprise. The old Indian looked at Sara with wonder. "Tall Woman Running, this is Simon Kenton, the famous scout."

Kenton stood up slowly. He looked very tired. He stared at Sara without a flicker of recognition.

"He will be stripped and forced to run the gauntlet!" announced the old man loudly. "If he falls, Barking Dog will beat him to death with his war club! Tall Woman Running will strike the first blow to start the gauntlet!"

The entire village crowded into the long double line and waited in silence. Several children could not stop swishing their blackberry switches. Kenton was dragged, naked, to the starting line. All Sara could see was his shiny bottom in front of her. She wanted to run away. The old man saw her hesitate. "Strike, daughter!" he shouted. "Or I will set Barking Dog on him!"

Sara raised her blackberry switch and swatted her Uncle Ned on the behind with all of her strength. He gave a yelp and ran like a deer down the long double line. The switches rose and fell, but he ran on, blood streaming down his white legs. After several club strikes, he staggered, but he never fell. At last, he reached the edge of the pool and fell in with a great splash, as all of the villagers cheered. When he came up in the water and saw them cheering, he started laughing. He climbed out of the water and shook himself like a great bear.

They then all had a feast, eating the turkeys he had been carrying home when the Indians descended on him.

That evening, the Indians built a huge fire in the pit, and Sara and the cats and Joey were honored guests. Simon Kenton came by to thank Sara for giving him such a good start.

Sara stared at him. "But … you're my uncle Ned," she insisted.

The huge frontiersman looked at her solemnly. "I am Simon Kenton; you are Tall Woman Running, the most lovely of all of the lovely Shawnee princesses. I am honored to know you. If I am to be your uncle Ned, I am also honored, but that must be in another life."

With that, Joey figured it was high time to end all of this, so he climbed up on the lap and then ran up the leather blouse of Tall Woman Running, and, hanging onto an ermine tail, offered her the ruby glass once more. Hesitantly she looked through its brilliant ruby glow and saw that she was sitting in a deserted clearing with a little mouse and three cats sitting in a circle around her. Somewhere on the long journey home in the dark, Joey lost the ruby glass. He went back to look for it many times but never found it again.

Adventure Number 9:

Joey Travels Deep into the Bob Marshall Wilderness

Joey was twenty mouse years old when he traveled into the Bob Marshall Wilderness. He was, of course, quite mature and experienced by this time. All of his previous travels had been  pretty tame compared with this adventure, even if some incidents had been exciting and even dangerous, as, for example the visit to the prairie dog town. He would never forget that day!

The journey to the Bob Marshall Wilderness came about as part of a great adventure out to the West in the motor home. J. D. and Colin, two of Joey's favorite humans, were traveling with the farmer this time. Both grandchildren of the farmer, these were big, rough guys. They didn't bother all that much with mouse language, either. They sometimes played catch with Joey, pretending that they were going to drop him, but they never did.

Colin came from Michigan. He was taller than J. D. and had dark brown hair and sometimes a mean look. J. D. was light-haired and sunny, but he was every bit as tough as Colin. They had been invited along by the farmer because this was a wilderness adventure and the farmer wanted his two oldest grandsons there to help keep himself and Granny safe. They also were a big help in sharing the driving as well as setting up camp.

They wanted to sleep out in a tent all the time, rather than inside the motor home. Joey liked that; he could come and go as he pleased, and he didn't have to worry about making a mess. He chewed a (very small) hole in the bottom corner of J. D.'s sleeping bag so he could crawl in, no matter how late he came back after a night out in the campsites. And he always found plenty of leftover crackers and peanuts for a snack before he went to sleep.

They had turned toward the real wilderness of Montana when they left the interstate highway at Missoula. They were headed north, along the Mission Mountains. A river twisted and turned this way and that, and the afternoon sun reflected first from sparkling riffles and then a broad flash from a deep pool. Piled high at the sharp bends in the river were huge banks of rocks. The stones were scoured smooth and round by uncounted years of free-running, crystal-clear water. They seemed to glow in the slanting sunlight; some were dark red, most were dark brown, and a few were black. Cottonwood trees crowded the banks where there was soil to hold them against spring floods. A waving net of insects rose into the sunlight from the surface of the river rising and falling in the current of unseen breezes.

Joey climbed through the motor home as it roared along, following his usual paths behind the cabinets to the television set at the front where he had gnawed a (very small) hole at the back. From there, he could reach a perch where he could see down the road, looking over the head of the driver. It was his best secret place. He knew that, when the sun started to get close to the horizon, they would be pulling into a camp, and Joey wanted a good look before he ventured out each night. The sun glinted off of the farmer's bald head; the glare interfered with Joey's view. He had to remind himself to stay awake. He had eaten a snack of pretzels from the picnic table after lunch and was very sleepy. He didn't want to fall asleep and have someone turn on the television set when he was in there!

"The reason this place is wilderness," said the farmer to J. D., who was riding "shotgun" beside him in the passenger seat, "is that everybody was afraid of it. There was a terrible fever that raged up and down this valley. The Indians knew all about it, and the pioneers found out about it soon enough. The squaws called it black fever or black death. It was a disease from the ticks that lived here. If anyone gets any tick bites on this trip, I want to know about it right away."

Up in the television set, Joey looked himself over carefully. He didn't see any ticks, and he found only one flea.

J. D. seemed to know all about this tick business. "Granddad, if the Indians had had antibiotics back then, they would probably be here lifting your scalp right now."

The farmer just laughed. Joey didn't think it was too funny. He didn't like the idea of some Indian lifting his mouse scalp.

They made camp in the dark just outside a small town named Hungry Horse. J. D. and Colin pitched their tent, and, after they had spread their sleeping bags, Joey slipped inside. He didn't like all of the talk about ticks and scalping and everything, so he decided he would stay in the tent that night and not go out looking around. Mice are very superstitious.

Early in the morning, they broke camp (but not before Joey had snatched a piece of pancake from beside the campfire) and headed down the east side of Hungry Horse Reservoir. The water was smooth and calm over the lake, but not the road beside it! They bumped and banged, throwing Joey around so much he was afraid he was going to be tossed out onto Granny's lap, where she was riding in the passenger seat. That would not do at all! Joey suspected that Granny knew that he was around. She had found her chewed-up straw hat when she cleaned out the closets after the last trip, and since then, she had talked about mousetraps. Fortunately the farmer didn't seem to pay any attention.

It took them all morning to reach Spotted Bear Ranch, which would be the base camp for their adventure. It more than made

up for all of the rough road! At the lodge they were served a lunch of ham sandwiches and dill pickles on rye bread—all of which Joey particularly liked. An added bonus—there were no cats around!

J. D. and Colin didn't eat nearly as much lunch as usual because of the camp cook. It wasn't that they didn't like the cook or the cooking; in fact, it was just the opposite. The cook, named Sarah, looked to be about nineteen human-years old. She was tall and very slender, with dark-brown eyes and long black hair. Joey thought she was about the most beautiful girl he had ever seen, and he had seen plenty. J. D. and Colin apparently thought so as well. They were a lot more polite than usual, and there was no rough stuff. Joey wondered if Sarah spoke mouse. She just looked as if she would.

Sarah had a soft voice and she teased the boys while she served them, telling them that, on the trail, they would have to serve themselves—and gather wood for the camp as well. That was when J. D. and Colin realized that she was going with them. Boy did that perk them up! Joey noticed that afternoon that they had both taken showers and were wearing clean clothes.

So there were four "sports." Joey soon learned that that is what the guides called people whom they were taking into the Bob Marshall. They were the farmer and Granny and J. D. and Colin— and of course Joey, but he didn't count. Joey was hiding in the pocket of J. D.'s wool shirt. In addition, there were two fishing guides and a tall, awkward-looking boy wearing a leather hat with a huge brim. He managed the horses and mules. And, of course, there was Sarah. Sarah and Granny were the only women and soon became fast friends.

The four mules carried the tents and camping gear, all of Sarah's food, pots, pans, a small collapsible tin oven, fishing gear, and three deflated orange rubber rafts—all tied down tightly.

Old Whiskey

There were eight horses, including the horse the guides assigned to Granny. The horse was named Old Whiskey. She was a huge white horse with brown and black splotches, called a "paint," and enormous blue eyes that glared at Granny with instant dislike. The feeling was mutual. The guides seemed to think this was funny.

Sarah told Granny that Whiskey was the safest horse in the string, but that didn't help very much.

The boy who ran the string had an Adam's apple that bobbed up and down as he shouted at the animals. The guides called him Gootch. He was as crazy about Sarah as all the rest of them.

Joey had found a large piece of pork chop beside the grill as they were saddling up, and he had to run fast to get up J. D.'s leg before J. D. swung up onto his horse. The horse shied away when it saw Joey, causing Gootch to yell at it. Fortunately, Gootch didn't see Joey. J. D. stuffed a Kleenex into his shirt pocket and Joey stirred it around and made himself comfortable. They had done this many times.

They were ready to start, and they were all on their horses except for Sarah. The head guide, a man older than J. D. or Colin but younger than the farmer, cupped his hands toward the lodge and shouted, "Come on, Saca-ja-wea! The string's leaving and we ain't got any cook!"

That was how Joey learned that the guides teased Sarah, nicknaming her after a famous Indian girl who had been a guide for some of the pioneers when they were trying to find their way through these mountains. Sarah came running out of the lodge, dressed in jeans and a dark red canvas blouse, with a red neckerchief flopping around her neck. The eye of every man in the string was on her. She ignored them and swung up on her horse with ease and smiled at Granny.

Jake, the head guide, turned in his saddle and shouted toward the back of the string, "Gootch, Saca-ja-wea is up from her nap! Now we don't need to worry about getting lost!"

Somewhere behind them, Gootch cracked a whip with a sound like a rifle shot. "Move 'em out!" he shouted, and they were on their way into the wilderness.

It was not easy going. The horses labored up steep slopes on a narrow crooked trail and then around the edge of the mountainsides where the rocky path overlooked huge rock slides, always above the river which wound below them. There were long stretches of white water and huge rocks separated by long, deep pools of transparent green water that spilled into the next set of rapids. When the horses descended a long, narrow, tortuous slope, they braced their front legs with each careful step, correcting for the smallest loose pebble. They were sure-footed—and bored. Whenever they could, they would snatch leaves from the shrubs and branches,

chewing and twisting their heads from side to side, and they had to be

forced into the stream where it could be forded, the icy water reaching the cinch straps beneath their bellies.

The guides were relaxed and seemed to be enjoying themselves, as they pointed out various peaks or a golden eagle perched on a lichen-covered rock. The "sports," on the other hand, clung to their reins and gripped the sides of the horses with their knees, using all of their strength and wondered how long this was going to last.

They made camp in the late afternoon, just as the sun was rimming the edge of a mountain to the west. The campsite was a large meadow elevated twenty feet above the level of the river and bordered by a huge gravel bank. A kingfisher scolded as they arrived, turning swiftly downstream and still chattering at them until it disappeared around a bend.

The campsite was clean and tidy. Except for the flattened grass where the tents were pitched and the fire ring, it would have been

Granny and Jake

difficult to know it had ever been used by the outfitters.

J. D. and Colin crawled stiffly off of their horses and huddled with the guides. Then they helped unpack the gear and search for firewood.

The farmer and Granny sank down beside each other on a log by the fire pit, looking worse for wear. The second guide, a guy named Pete, went off to dig a latrine. Soon a fire was crackling against the cold air that was sweeping down the meadow from the snowfields high above them. Pans were clattering and clanking, and the tiny tin oven had been unfolded and set by the side of the fire. Sarah was very busy—and very bossy concerning the firewood! Soon the smell of cooking filled the air. None of the "sports" could remember being so hungry.

J. D. and Colin couldn't believe what Sarah cooked for dinner! First, she insisted on doing it all herself. Granny was not allowed to lift a finger. Sarah explained, with her beautiful smile, that Granny was a guest and not there to cook for hungry men!

A large supply of deadfall had been brought in from the woods, cut with a small saw, and fed under two large wire grates. Sarah maneuvered two huge skillets around on them, moving away to mix batter, then back for some adjustment or other. The oven was placed over separate coals to heat. A huge coffee pot steamed on one side. The smells drew everyone in like a magnet.

Darkness was falling swiftly, and it turned very cold, but Sarah was sweating heavily as she labored over the campfire. Her forehead glistened, and a strand of dark hair fell across it as she bent over the fire. She kept brushing it back impatiently. There was a dark streak of sweat down the back of her canvas shirt and dark spots under her arms. J. D. couldn't keep his eyes off of her. Colin was smiling at him slyly. Colin had a steady girlfriend back in Michigan, where he had been a big football star. But he knew that J. D. was on the prowl, and he was laughing as he watched J. D. and Sarah. The guides and Gootch seemed not to notice.

How they feasted! One of the huge skillets contained two inches of hamburger, toasted brown and covered with two inches of mashed potatoes, dark brown on top from the searing heat, and laced across with melted cheese. The other skillet was filled to the brim with carrots, sliced onions, and strips of fried bacon. The coffee was black and strong, and from the tiny oven came small biscuits as brown as a pine knot and hot enough to burn the tongue. Sarah refilled the oven three times while they were eating. Then three huge pies were cut up for dessert.

J. D. thought he ate a lot, but he couldn't hold a candle to Colin, who ate enough for three people, yet there was more than plenty. When they all were finished, Sarah gathered the tin plates and utensils in a porcelain-coated wash basin, threw in a squirt bottle of soap and a wire brush, picked up the two large skillets in her free hand, and turned to Granny where she sat comfortably on a small folding camp stool.

"Make sure all these animals stay where you can see them," she said to Granny. As she smiled, her white teeth shone in the firelight. "I'm off to the river and a bath. This is a fishing trip—not a carnival show!" She laughed as she disappeared into the darkness. Granny counted noses and made certain the count stayed the same.

Joey did so well scavenging scraps and scrapings by the fire that he crawled into the tent with his belly so full the hair was sticking out on the front side.

When J. D. stirred awake, it was ice cold outside the down sleeping bag. He could see frost on the inside of the nylon wall of the small tent. When he opened the fly, he saw that the ground was covered with heavy frost. There was smoke coming from the campfire, and Sarah was busy with breakfast. Jake stood beside her with a steaming cup of coffee gripped in his big hands. He was laughing at something she had said. J. D. could see the sky bright behind the eastern ridge of mountains. Colin was stirring beside him. He knew it was going to be a fine day.

As they started the morning ride, they climbed a steep rough trail. The mountains pressed tightly against the stream, which ran narrower and faster over huge rocks. Down the steep hillsides ran small sparkling tributaries to the river. When they crossed them on the narrow, high trails, it was slippery and treacherous. Osprey and kingfishers worked below them, hunting along the river, occasionally dropping with folded wings. There would then be a splash in the sunlight, and the bird would usually emerge with a small trout. On a far meadow, the riders spotted a young grizzly. Gootch shouted at the horses and mules and cracked the whip again and again to quiet them.

That afternoon, they reached their float camp, where they unpacked everything, set up, and inflated the rafts. After another huge supper, the fire was built up and the "sports" watched in amazement as Gootch and the guides repacked the mules and strung the horses together. Then the tall lanky boy came over to the fire to say good-bye.

Colin couldn't control his curiosity. "You aren't starting back down that trail *alone*, are you Gootch?" he asked.

"Oh, I ain't alone, Mr. Colin, I got all them horses and mules, sometimes even a grizzly!" He was smiling and very proud.

"At night?" asked Colin.

"Yes, sir," replied Gootch. "Me and them horses really make good time. We'll go all night, be home late tomorrow afternoon, most likely."

"Wow," was all Colin could say.

The tall, skinny boy with his huge hat pulled low and his collar turned up against the cold was a sight they would never forget. He touched the broad brim of the hat briefly to Granny and then to Sarah, swung up into the saddle of the lead horse, and disappeared into the darkness. The jingle of the string could be heard briefly until it was lost against the sound of the stream.

"Well," said Jake into the silence, "the horse trip is all over. I know you all feel real bad about that. Folks, the only way home is down this little stream."

That was not the end of the surprises. After breakfast, when all of the fishing gear was ready and the dry flies for the day had been selected, the guides went down to the edge of the stream and loaded the largest orange raft full of the camping gear, the cooking gear, and personal duffels. Then Sarah calmly walked out on the gravel bar where the raft was beached, crawled in, and shoved off into the swift water. Soon she was bobbing up and down in the nearest set of rapids. She quickly disappeared around a sharp bend. J. D. stared after the raft. He turned back to Jake, who was lighting a black cheroot.

"Where's she going?" he demanded.

"Down the river, I reckon," replied Jake laconically.

"Aren't we staying together?"

"We'll fish together, sort of, make our own lunch. We'll meet Sarah at the evening camp."

"She's going down that river with all of that stuff piled up in there *all alone*?" demanded J. D. He didn't care that he sounded silly.

"That's her job, mister. She does it a way I like real well." Jake

considered J. D. for a minute, then decided he liked him. "She's a college kid," he continued after a long pull on the cheroot. "Over at Oregon State. Works here summers. This is her third summer. We never had any better, man, woman, young, or old. Always one step ahead of the boys, never mean to them. I wouldn't trade her for ten year's growth—if I needed any."

"I don't think she should be in that boat alone," countered J. D. "In the first place, it's overloaded. In the second place, she may be strong, but she's not *that* strong."

J. D. couldn't believe what he was hearing himself saying—telling this man how to run his business.

"Well," replied Jake after another pause, "I think I'll let *you* tell her that." He walked off across the rough stones. Joey thought he could hear him chuckling as he went.

They fished all day long, all dry flies on barbless hooks. All of the cutthroat trout they caught were released except for a small mess they grilled for lunch on a glacial deposit lining the shore. They passed when a boat had a fish in one of the deep pools, only to be passed up again in turn. The fish were wild and aggressive, slashing up from the depths to strike, then twisting, jumping, fighting until exhausted. Once caught, they were carefully revived, held upright, and coaxed to swim in the freezing water until they gave a final quick twist and darted back into the hidden depths.

They lost count of the number of fish hooked and released. Joey had a rough day in J. D.'s pocket with all of that twisting and moving, but the wool gave him a good grip. He did have several close calls when J. D. leaned far over the side of the raft to net a fish. He was pleased that he could see through the *(tiny)* hole he had chewed in J. D.'s shirt pocket so he did not have to stick his head out. He could see far down, past a long stretch of rapids, Sarah's large orange raft, pulled up onto a wide, sandy beach. He was happy to see that; he was tired of being mashed around in all of those fish fights.

Late that evening, as the sun was setting, Sarah went down to the shore to scrub the supper dishes. J. D. followed her down to the beach and walked over to where she had started scrubbing a skillet with a handful of sand. She seemed surprised to see him and stood up to face him. "Evening, J. D.," she said quietly. "Is something wrong?"

"No," said J. D. "I mean yes ..." J. D. scratched his head. "I guess I don't know," he admitted finally. She was nearly as tall as he was. Her face was calm.

"I don't like you riding in this river all alone in that overloaded raft!" he finally said. "I know it's none of my business. I can't help it."

"It's my job."

"It's not worth it."

"I like the people I come out here with, J. D., both these guys I work with and you people. I have fun. I worry about the raft sometimes, especially down by the falls, but Jake is always extra careful down there. We usually make the last stretch fast; people are often tired of fishing by then, and the bottom stretch is so rough the fishing isn't all that good, anyway."

"I want to ride down with you tomorrow—all day," said J. D.

Sarah looked at him strangely. "J. D., I try to never get serious about anybody out here, you know what I mean? Guys come out here to work, or you people come out here to have a good time. I don't think it's wise to get serious. That way no one gets hurt, know what I mean?"

"I think this is different," said J. D. simply.

She looked at him for a long time. Then she reached up and put her hand along his cheek. Her fingers were cold from the icy water. "Give me a break, J. D.," she said quietly. "All I know about you is you're a good-looking guy with good manners. And we are out here in the boondocks where its a little crazy. Not good enough. Give me a break. You know even less about me."

"I know you go to Oregon State and are one hell of a cook," replied J. D. "That's enough for me."

"No, it's not."

"I'm not going to let this go, Sarah."

She turned back to the stream and bent down over the tin pans. She picked up a fresh handful of sand. "You will have to ask Jake if you want to float with me tomorrow."

"I already have."

"So?"

"It's up to you ... according to Jake."

When he heard that, Joey crossed one paw over the other in J. D.'s pocket. Mice do that when they hear a lie.

Sarah started scrubbing. "Fine. Be ready early. I like to be off first."

Joey thought it was pretty crazy, feeling a big guy like J. D. dancing a jig and acting silly on his way back to the camp.

That is how it happened that J. D. and Sarah rode a long stretch of the South Fork of the Flathead River—J. D. in the front of the huge raft and Sarah perched on the back rim, steering with a large sweep. She guided the raft through the rapids, then swept it powerfully back and forth as they coasted across the large pools. Cutthroat scattered from under their shadow and raced for safety in the riffles. The silence was complete except for the chattering of kingfishers and the occasional loud croak of a raven from the top of a tall pine tree.

At lunchtime, Sarah steered the raft onto a gravel bank. J. D. hopped out and pulled the raft up on the rocks until it was firmly beached. Sarah stepped out of the back, into the shallow water, and stretched. "String up that fly rod of yours, Mr. Sport, and catch us some lunch." she ordered.

J. D. strung the rod, tied on a small fly, and waded out, casting upstream. As he waded he kept looking back to the shore. He saw Sarah gather a few tufts of dead grass and press it around some-

thing. Then there was a twirling motion between her two hands, after which she held the tuft of grass up, blew on it—and it immediately burst into flames! He couldn't believe his eyes. He thought that kind of stuff was for sporting-goods shows; he didn't believe that *anybody* started fires that way anymore. He crossed the riffle at the bottom of the pool, the strong current forcing him to pay attention, and, casting into the shady side, he was soon catching fish.

He brought back three twelve-inch cutthroat. Sarah had the tiny fire going at the water's edge. It gave off only a small wisp of smoke. She gutted and cleaned the fish, threw the entrails into the stream, and grilled the trout on a small round mesh set over a small circle of rocks. Soon they were picking off small strips of sizzling fish and eating with their fingers. There followed large chunks of brown bread and pieces of cheese, hard as a rock, which Sarah sliced with her hunting knife.

They sat for a long time in the hot sun, comparing notes, finding those small details that make a difference, the murmurs going on so long that Joey became overheated. Finally, he crawled out of J. D.'s pocket to get some air. Sarah stared at him. "You have a pet mouse!" she exclaimed.

"Joey," replied J. D. "Mostly he's a pet for the smaller kids. But he's hard to leave back on the farm. Want to hold him?"

Without being asked, Joey ran down J. D.'s extended arm and leaped across the space, landing on Sarah's jeans and quickly running up to her throat. She didn't even flinch. She picked Joey up and stared at him, smiling. She opened her hand, and Joey stood up on his back legs in her palm. "How neat!" Sarah exclaimed.

"Joey's my buddy," said J. D., extending his hand. Joey hopped back aboard. "He's the one who thought I should ride down the river with you."

Joey wanted to cross his feet but thought it was not a good idea under the circumstances.

Sarah looked at J. D. "Then I guess he's my friend, too," she said. She shook her head, making the long, dark hair swirl around her shoulders. "The Indians have a legend about this river, J. D. They say this is a place where their young learn to love one another." She busied herself brushing the tiny fire into the river, after which she washed her hands and dried them on her jeans. When she stood up her face was very serious.

She turned suddenly and went back into the brush. She was gone for a longer time than they expected, and when she reappeared, she had a few blackberries in her hand and a blackened root about the size of a man's finger. "Eat the berries," she stated.

J. D. gulped them down.

"Now chew on the root, and when your mouth puckers up, spit it out."

J. D. chewed and spit. It was really sour!

"That's bitterroot," explained Sarah. Sarah smiled at J. D., teasing him with her eyes. "Now, J. D., as soon as you go kill a grizzly with a spear, I can be your squaw."

J. D. had a smile few women could resist. "I will need a couple of days to find a spear," he replied. They both laughed and then shoved the raft off of the beach, clambered aboard, and were whisked away down the river.

The afternoon was more of the same, except that the river was growing ominously in power and deception. Huge rocks loomed out of nowhere, with enormous eddies around them. Occasionally, the raft, with its heavy load, would scrape over a hidden boulder, almost throwing them off. They passed ever-larger waterfalls cascading into the river; beside one, a large herd of mule deer raced away from them toward the woods.

J. D., riding in front, spotted the campsite long before they arrived. It was in a huge grove of cottonwoods, and, as they drew nearer, he could see areas where tents had been pitched throughout the long summer. There was not a speck of litter anywhere. Sarah worked the sweep against the powerful current to finally cross over to the huge bank of gravel, where they grounded. The raft scraped noisily up the bank, pushed by the surge of water behind them as they slowed to a stop.

"What's first?" asked J. D. after he had secured the raft to a large cottonwood twenty feet away.

"You go fishing, J. D. I'll unload. I do it every trip."

J. D. pretended to be puzzled. He slid his fingers through his hair. "What sort of woman," he asked, "would feed someone bitterroot and then refuse to let him help her with all of this junk?"

Sarah laughed at that. "Okay, my fine fellow, all of it goes up to the fire ring, sooner or later."

He couldn't believe how heavy some of the boxes and duffels were. He lugged them up the steep bank and over to the fire ring. She matched him step for step. He realized that if she was doing all of this alone, she would be hard-pressed to finish by the time the other boats arrived.

He watched as Sarah opened a cardboard box and shook out some few remaining smoking crystals of dry ice. She held up a glistening package of frozen steaks. "This is it," she announced proudly. "The final dinner. Tomorrow is a three-hour stretch down to the foot bridge above the falls. So tonight we celebrate and get ready to say good-bye."

J. D. felt like someone had just run him through with a javelin.

Sarah reached into her duffel, and out came a large towel and a metal soap container. "Thanks to you, J. D., I can take a bath before the rest get here."

She watched J. D. look back and forth from the camp to the river. "Tell you what," she said. "Take that trail over there and keep at it until you get to the top of the cliff. If you see them coming, give a loud whistle!" She turned and walked toward the river.

J. D. did as he was told. It was a long, hot, hard climb to the top. He looked as far up the river as he could. It was empty, except for an osprey building a nest on the top of a dead snag. Then, in spite of himself, he looked back down the river.

Sarah was waist-deep in the water. Her bare back was toward him, and she was washing her hair, the muscles rippling along her back as she scrubbed. Her jeans and shirt were washed and stretched over nearby bushes. He looked back up the river. He wouldn't have been able to whistle if a herd of elephants had been coming down the river. When he looked back, she was standing up and stepping into her jeans. He watched as she pulled on the shirt and tied the tails at her waist. She didn't look his way. When he thought about it, he realized that she knew he had looked. This must be her way of telling him he was a special person. And that his watching her from up there had been no different than if he had been watching the osprey working at feeding her young.

After the other rafts came bobbing and twisting down the river and voices floated out to him about all of the fishes that had been caught, J. D. walked away from the camp. He climbed the hill again and sat up there with Joey and thought about Sarah. Jake whistled him down for the steaks and fried potatoes.

When he crawled into his tent, Colin raised himself up on an elbow and said, "Man, you have it really bad, you know that?"

J. D. didn't reply.

The final day's float was designed to be short. Jake gave a brief speech before they shoved off, explaining there was a large cataract as the river left the mountains after it ran through a narrow gorge. The current became unmanageable, he explained, flowing through the gorge, and there was a large boom of empty drums across the river, well upstream of the overhead foot bridge. They were to disembark above the boom, where their personal belongings would be taken across to the lodge. All of the rest of the baggage would be taken care of later that afternoon. He didn't mention it, but the idea was to get the guests packed up and away before nightfall so the staff could take a well-earned rest.

Spotted Bear Ranch was located where it was because of the cataract. The footbridge was a flimsy suspension bridge looking down on the steel cables that secured the line of barrels. The barrels formed a barrier to any passage beyond that point in the river. Before they rounded the final bend, Jake was already worried about the water level and the strength of the current. He saw J. D. and Sarah swing around the bend, and, to his horror as his raft also swung around, he saw there was no boom in place! He stood up in the raft and screamed over the noise of the river, "Sarah! The boom is gone! *Get out!*"

The two people in equipment raft seemed not to hear—although Sarah was already working hard on the sweep, trying to force the raft toward the shore. It was responding slowly. As he watched, Jake realized that the raft was not going to make the shore. The noise of the falls was rising fast from down the river. "*Sarah! J. D.!*" he screamed, "*To hell with the stuff! Bail out!*"

Sarah was still struggling to beach the raft, but they were still twenty feet from the shore. J. D. looked back at the following raft. He could hear nothing, but when he saw Jake, he realized that something was terribly wrong.

Sarah threw the handle of the sweep away and struggled toward the set of oars in the center of the raft. She started to fight them into their oarlocks so she could row them ashore.

J. D. took one look at the river and another look back at the following raft. He tackled Sarah at the waist, sending them both over the side and into the river. They turned and twisted along the bottom, scraping across rocks. They stumbled upright, fell, struggled some more, and, half swimming, half walking, moved toward the shore, hanging onto each other—until suddenly, Colin and Jake appeared, waist–deep, in front of them, pulling them, exhausted, to safety. "Out of the pool, kids," said Colin. "Rest period. Time for the adults."

They sank down on the rocks and rested as the last raft beached, and the farmer and Granny ran up, having watched helplessly from upriver. Then they heard a crash as the first raft went over the cataract. J. D. reached into his shirt pocket and withdrew a soaked and terrified Joey. Even Granny smiled when J. D. started wiping Joey off with his wet handkerchief.

As they walked across the bridge toward the lodge, they could see the debris of the first raft scattered below, where the river spread out as it meandered toward the reservoir. The raft was lying upside down on a huge rock.

Sarah was watching J. D.'s face as they walked. She took his hand in hers. "C'mon, J. D. don't look so serious. Think of all the girls out there who love you."

That made J. D.'s chest hurt. What hurt was his realization that this was the end of the trip. What hurt was the knowledge that he might never see her again. He knew he would never forget her—the woman the guides loved to tease and call Saca-ja-wea.

Adventure Number 10:

Joey Makes Headlines in The San Francisco Examiner

In Joey's twenty-fifth mouse-year, Joey went to San Francisco. It was quite an eventful trip—they had visited Yellowstone National Park and taken a float fishing trip down the Madison River.

On the drive to San Francisco, they came across the desert, through some high, snowy mountains, and past a wonderful, deep, blue lake. Joey had very little idea where they were, although he really liked the scenery.

Dan

When they arrived in San Francisco, the farmer had a difficult time navigating in the motor home because the streets were very narrow and there were large, steep hills with cars parked all over. Added to that, streetcars ran up and down the hills, their bells always clanging away.

Joey was stuck with only Buck for company for three days in a big parking lot, while the farmer and Granny and Dan and Kelly went off without them to stay in a big hotel on Union Square. From there, they went off to see all of the sights!

Joey considered slipping down out of the wheel well to see some sights himself, but no sooner had he hit the parking lot blacktop, a bit after midnight, when he saw a huge wharf rat that sniffed and then started running toward him. Joey scuttled back up the wheel and was soon next to Buck—who was snoring away up in his favorite place by the driver's seat.

After that it was pure boredom. Buck spent the time snoring and getting up to eat when the farmer came back to walk and feed him. Joey was left with only a part of Buck's dull dog food to eat. Joey had to keep reminding himself that anyplace that had wharf rats that size also had to have some really mean cats.

The only excitement Joey had during the whole three days was when someone tried the door in the middle of the night. Buck jumped up with such a terrible bellow that Joey fell off of the warm converter where he was sleeping. All they heard after that were footsteps running away.

It did get very foggy outside every night, and Joey could sometimes hear foghorns in the far distance. He had heard the farmer say that they were going to go up to some giant redwood forest and see the ocean, so Joey contented himself with wondering what an ocean looked like.

Finally they were on their way! It was afternoon, and Dan and Kelly bounced into the motor home wearing new San Francisco T-shirts. Soon, they were eating pretzels at the breakfast table and drinking orange soda. Joey's mouth was watering in anticipation of something tasty after all of that dog food, and he watched through a crack, noting where each crumb fell. By the time he made his way through the insulation to see where they were headed, the sun was setting over a huge bank of fog that was rolling in from a glittering expanse of water.

They were on a huge bridge that seemed to go on as far as Joey could see—toward a distant shoreline. So this was an ocean!

Wow! He could see seals playing on the rocks below Golden Gate Bridge as they started out over the span of the bridge itself.

They were rolling along at a fast pace. The sea was sweeping in high rollers far below them. Then, the flashing lights of a police cruiser sent waves of blue and red across the motor home, and they ground to a stop right behind the cruiser, as a policeman held up his hand to indicate they should stop. The policeman then made a sign waggling his fingers across his throat and pointed at the motor, so the farmer cut the engine, and there they sat.

Joey looked to the side and saw a man at the edge of the steel walkway. He had crawled up on the railing and was hanging out over the edge, holding on to a steel cable and screaming that he was going to jump! Another policeman was shouting at him, but the man kept shouting back not to come any closer or he would jump.

Joey was never able to explain what happened next. All he could recall was that he had run as fast as he could for the wheel well and then scampered along the steel walkway, where the gaps in the mesh were almost as wide as his body. He had run up on the railing to the leg of the man, who was now swinging back and forth out over the edge. He realized that there was a very strong wind blowing, and it could easily blow him away. He ran up the leg of the man's pants and, finally, up a smelly shirt to where he could see the man's face.

Though the man was not very old, he looked old. His clothes were messy, and his hair was long and tangled. The last rays of the sun turned his face a dark red, and his eyes were even more red and he looked very unhappy. Even so, Joey thought that he looked like a nice man; even more important, Joey was almost certain he spoke mouse. Joey had no idea how he knew this. If anyone would know, it would be Fred.

"Hi there!" Joey shouted over the howl of the wind.

The man looked down at Joey. He had a short, very dirty beard, and he had to look over it to see Joey. Now his eyes appeared dark brown and very sad. Joey thought that the man had been crying. "Hi," he replied to Joey. It was more polite than anything.

Joey nodded toward the policeman who was shouting at them. "I think he wants you to get back on the other side of the railing," said Joey.

"I'm not getting back anywhere!" the man shouted at the cop. "I'm going to jump any minute." Cars were backing up behind the motor home, and horns were honking.

Joey crawled out to the man's shoulder and tried to stand up to look more important. A gust of wind almost blew him away, though, and he had to drop down and hang on. "Big Dan says that people who jump off bridges lose a lot more than they think," screamed Joey. He was afraid to look down, knowing he would only see the breakers far below.

"Lose? What's to lose?" shouted the man.

The shrink

Joey had to think fast. He swept a paw toward the horizon. "Look at that sunset!" he shouted. "Look at it! You would miss all of those!"

The man looked at Joey more closely. Joey did his best to look wise. "Who's this Big Dan, anyway?" he asked, as he swung out wide again. Joey was sure he was going to let go.

"He's a shrink!" shouted Joey. "He's the father of that little boy over there in that big motor home.

84

You're going to make that little boy cry a lot if you let go of that cable."

"He don't even know me!"

"He knows me, you idiot! I'm his mouse!" That was sort of a lie, but Joey didn't think that crossing his feet was the right thing to do under the circumstances.

For the first time, the man smiled. "Don't try that stuff on me, mouse. I've been to the shrinks. All they ever say is to get in touch with your inner self and all of that ..." He said a bad word.

"No, it's not like that," argued Joey. "Would I come up here like this if I didn't care about you?"

The man looked very sad. "Well, I suppose ... but you're only a mouse, you know." He realized what he had said and seemed to be trying to say something better.

Out of the corner of his eye, Joey saw some people with cameras and several men in white uniforms sneaking up the walkway toward the man, who was now looking down at Joey and not paying attention. Joey decided to take a terrible chance. He jumped from the man's shoulder right into the thick beard. It really smelled bad! It almost made Joey sick.

"Hey," shouted the man. "What are you doing? You're going to go with me, mouse, if you don't get off me!" He let go of the cable, and Joey was sure that was the end.

Two huge arms surrounded the man's legs and stripped him off of the railing, pulling him onto the deck. Joey stuck his head out of the beard. Cameras were clicking and bright lights flashed everywhere. "Hey, look," a cop yelled. "That homeless man has a pet mouse!" More cameras clicked.

"C'mon Eddie," shouted the cop's partner. "Let's get this traffic moving so they can load that nut into an ambulance."

Joey panicked. The cop was signaling the motor home to get moving. The farmer started the motor with a huge roar. Joey ran as fast as his legs could carry him, but by the time he was at the curb, the huge motor home was rolling past him. He ducked under the back wheel, and, just before it squashed him, he jumped up and shot through his entry place. All of a sudden he was safe! He could hear Buck sniffing from within the coach. Joey guessed that Buck had probably watched it all and was worried.

The next day, they were at a place called Muir Woods, where there were the biggest trees Joey had ever seen. When everyone else went off for a hike, Joey decided to see what he could find in some of the trash cans. He was just about to carry off a delicious piece of discarded hamburger bun when his eye fell on a copy of *The San Francisco Examiner*. There was a picture on the front page of the man swinging from the cable on the bridge. A huge headline said:

Man claims mouse's psychiatrist saved his life

In a second picture, right in the middle of the man's beard, stood Joey. The photo had been taken right after the medic had tackled the man, and he was lying on his back on the sidewalk. The story said that the man's name was Stewart and he had been a stockbroker once and was now homeless. The story also said that the man kept raving that a mouse had come to him on the bridge and talked him into not jumping. The reporter had written that nobody believed the man, but when they looked at the photographs, everybody was wondering whether it might be true. One of the policemen claimed he also had seen the mouse. A man two cars back in the line said he had seen a sea gull deliver the mouse and put the mouse into the man's beard, and he was sure it was some sort of miracle.

That night, after everyone was asleep, Joey crept out into the cabin and told Buck all about it while he munched on some fresh chunks of pretzel. He really liked pretzels.

Adventure Number 11:

Joey Travels to the End of the Earth

When Joey learned that the farmer and Aunt Ruth were going to travel to the end of the earth, he immediately started to figure out how he could go along. The first problem was that Fred had told him that the earth was round, like a huge ball. Joey couldn't figure out, if the earth was round, how could it have an end at all. The more Joey tried to figure that out, the more confused he became. He finally gave up, telling himself that he didn't understand because he wasn't very good at math.

He started to hang out more at the farmhouse while the planning for the trip was underway. He soon learned that the idea was to go to see some very rare birds and animals in places that were often called "the end of the earth" because very few people had been to them. That made Joey even more determined to go; he was certain that very few mice had been to these places either.

Actually, it turned out to be easy. When Aunt Ruth came to finish her packing at the farm, Joey hopped up on the table and stood up on his hind legs. She knew right away what was up. Aunt Ruth was a teacher and lived in Michigan. Actually, she was Colin and Erin's mother and the farmer's daughter, but almost everyone else in the family called her Aunt Ruth. She had been very impressed with Joey's adventure on the Golden Gate Bridge and had even written for a copy of the photograph of Joey sticking his head out of Stewart's filthy beard. Teachers collect things like that, and Aunt Ruth collected everything. She also spoke mouse—though rather stiffly and with a funny accent.

So, when Joey hopped up on the table, she knew right away what he was after. "So, Joey," she guessed, "I think you are trying to hitch a ride with me to Indonesia."

Joey nodded vigorously, although he had no idea where Indonesia was.

"Do you get seasick?" asked Aunt Ruth.

Joey said he had never been seasick. Of course, he had never been to sea, either, but under the circumstances, he didn't think it was necessary to cross his feet.

The teacher went on packing—she was taking a lot of jungle stuff, along with binoculars and cameras and snorkel gear. Finally, she held up a half-empty roll of toilet paper. "Do you think you could ride half-way around the world inside this roll?" she asked. She was smiling mischievously.

She placed it on the table and Joey crawled inside. There was plenty of room. He hopped out and told Aunt Ruth that it would be just fine. "Just don't let the farmer catch you," Aunt Ruth cautioned. "I don't think he would approve."

So the next day, off they went. Joey was curled up inside the roll, and Aunt Ruth had placed it inside a large purse with her personal things, some medicines, and several rolls of film.

Joey learned a good lesson at the first airport: to stay quiet, no matter what happened. Joey had been bumping along inside the purse on a conveyor, when a man in a uniform picked up the purse and opened it and poked around. When he saw the roll of toilet paper, he was sort of embarrassed and put it back quickly. He handed the purse to Aunt Ruth and told her he hoped that she didn't need it for an emergency.

Aunt Ruth acted sort of offended and stalked off, but actually she was laughing and talking to Joey as she ran down the concourse to the airplane. Something similar happened before they got on the big airplane to fly over the ocean, except the men in uniforms didn't even bother to open the purse. It went through some sort of machine that took pictures right through the wall of the purse, and Joey heard one man laughing and saying to another man that Aunt Ruth was a crazy broad who had a stuffed mouse in her purse.

Then they spent a long, long time in the noisy airplane. Aunt Ruth fed Joey some great food and gave him some sips of soda from a thimble she was carrying (she had everything you could imagine in that purse), and she even carried him into the rest room several times and made him poop on a tissue. Joey didn't like doing those things with Aunt Ruth watching, but she was tough about it. Teachers can be pretty tough, especially about things like that.

Finally, they arrived at a port on a beautiful clear blue sea. There, they boarded a ship with tall spars that soon unfurled a magnificent billow of white sails. The ship moved into the setting sun. Aunt Ruth had transferred Joey to a shirt pocket. He chewed a (very small) hole so that he could see out.

That night, on the ship, they had a dinner of very spicy food, which Joey found that he liked very much. Afterward, they went to bed in a cabin where the farmer was also sleeping. This meant that Joey had to be very careful when he went out to explore. He was pleased to find there were no cats aboard and apparently no other mice—but he did find members of the crew, mostly small, brown men, sleeping on the open deck in the warm breeze. He was very careful not to wake them or be seen by the men up front, in the lighted cabin, who were steering the ship.

When Joey later looked back on it, the adventure seemed more like a dream than anything else. They sailed by day among jungle islands covered with thick green foliage. Thousands of birds roosted

there, some rising up in immense white flocks as they passed. Other huge birds, with big beaks, appeared over the canopy and then suddenly dropped down into it with harsh cries that echoed over the water.

Sometimes, the humans would get all dressed up in jungle clothes and go ashore in big red rubber rafts. They would enter the dark jungle, hike up stony trails, past huge trees, to places where they saw huge butterflies with bodies almost the size of Joey. They also saw all sorts of birds, including some that made loud croaking calls as they ran away into the darkness—Joey was astonished at these birds who couldn't fly!

The leader was a photographer and naturalist and he liked Aunt Ruth very much. Joey thought it was because most of the other travelers were the farmer's age. Sometimes the photographer took Aunt Ruth to places where the others would have found the going too rough. Joey suspected that the photographer spoke mouse, and it wasn't very long before the secret was out. Joey was then able (when others weren't around) to ride with his head sticking out of Aunt Ruth's pocket. This, of course, was much more comfortable, especially if there was a cool breeze blowing in from the ocean.

One day, they went in an ocean kayak to a small crevice in some huge black rocks. Inside was a huge cave filled with things that had a body like a mouse—except that, where Joey had front feet, they had wings! Their shrieks filled the air as they fluttered about in the darkness. The photographer called them "bats," and he was very proud of finding them. Joey realized that he had seen something like them back home, fluttering in the evening light down in the valley, but he had always assumed that they were birds. You really learn some neat stuff when you travel, Joey decided. He couldn't wait to tell Fred.

Some of the bats came very close; Joey felt almost as if the bats were diving on them. As Joey listened, he realized that their language was very similar to mouse, but he couldn't quite get it. He was sure that, if he had more time, he would be able to learn it and then be able to talk with the bats. But Aunt Ruth had seen enough, and they slipped out through the crevice into the brilliance of the afternoon sun.

On some of the larger islands, they met other humans, who were almost all dark brown in color and very thin. They ate strange foods, mostly a pasty, white food that Joey found that he didn't like, and coconut meat, which he liked very much. And then Joey saw the worst sight he had ever seen, anywhere—a pile of very large mice that had been roasted for somebody's dinner! Joey couldn't wait to get back to the ship after that one!

They also saw several snakes and a lot of monkeys, both of which gave Joey the creeps. Fortunately, the snakes and monkeys seemed to feel the same way about the humans, so Joey just kept himself tucked well down into Aunt Ruth's shirt pocket. Only when she told him that they'd gone away could she coax him back out.

Joey's favorite part of the trip was visiting a village where there was a large school for the children. Aunt Ruth was asked by the

teacher to say something to the class. Well, what did she do but pull Joey out of her pocket and sit him right in the center of a desk where they could all watch him! The children laughed and gathered around, and the photographer heard all of the noise and came and took a photograph of Joey standing up on his hind legs, looking important. Actually, that photograph caused a lot of trouble! But more about that later.

At the school, Joey ran into a bit of trouble. One of the little girls asked Aunt Ruth if she could have Joey as a pet. Joey's heart sank. He knew that Aunt Ruth was always giving things away to children. He knew that she had a big problem saying no to something like that. Aunt Ruth picked Joey up and held him in her palm, about an inch from her face. She was smiling at him, which worried him even more. "How about it, Joey?" she asked.

Joey didn't answer. Instead, he jumped straight into her pocket, burrowed as deep as he could, and decided he was going to hold on with his teeth, his claws—with everything he had! He heard Aunt Ruth laugh and then she stroked him through the cloth of the pocket. Joey knew he was safe, so he stuck his head out of the pocket, and all of the children laughed at him.

Soon it was time to leave the ship. Everyone was packing up, getting ready to dock and go to the airport for the long, long ride home.

The photographer had meant to give the photograph of Joey with the schoolchildren to Aunt Ruth, but he found that it had been packed by mistake and sent off to *National Geographic*, along with the photographs of rare species of birds and animals that the photographer had collected as an assignment for the magazine. Even worse, the photographer, as a joke for Aunt Ruth to take home, had labeled the photograph of Joey as "an indigenous mouse species discovered on Bok Island and therefore given the name *Muscus bokius*." Wow, what a fuss that caused!

Joey had a very narrow escape during the customs inspection when they arrived back in New York. The roll of toilet paper was no longer available to shield him. In fact, it had been used up one morning on a long jungle hike after a special (and extremely spicy) dinner on the ship. There hadn't even been enough on the roll to supply the needs of all of the birdwatchers.

Aunt Ruth had wisely decided that it would not do for Joey to remain in her shirt pocket as she went through customs, so she pulled Joey out of the pocket as they entered the big customs room, and she slipped him down the front of her shirt. Joey snuggled in, determined to keep very quiet. When Aunt Ruth approached the inspector, he looked over her passport, then looked her over, and finally he asked her if she had brought any plants, animals, or any other biological material back into the United States.

Aunt Ruth looked the inspector straight in the eye and said, "No."

Joey immediately crossed his feet to ward off the harm that he knew could come from telling a lie. There was a long pause while the inspector inspected Aunt Ruth's front. Joey didn't move again or breathe. Finally, the inspector waved her through.

It seemed like no time at all before they were at the airport in Columbus. and Jim, the policeman, was there to pick up the farmer and Aunt Ruth and take them home. As soon as the farmer dozed off in the back of the car, Joey hopped out and up on the dashboard, where he ran from one side to the other to get some exercise while the policeman and Aunt Ruth talked about the trip. Buck and Fred were waiting for Joey when the car pulled up the long lane and stopped. Joey rode deep in the fur of Buck's back to the barn, where Ruby and Charlie and several mice were waiting to hear all about Joey's trip to the end of the earth.

Adventure Number 12:

Joey Decides It is Time
to Start a Family

After Joey's photograph appeared in *National Geographic* and he was identified as a brand-new species of mouse, he became famous all over again. At the farm, there were young mice who often came by and asked him questions about things he didn't know anything about. It was sort of embarrassing.

Fred was jealous of all of the attention Joey was getting as an expert, but he always hung around, anyway, to hear whatever Joey had to say.

Joey heard him one day, down at the farmhouse, lecturing the other cats about hornbills, the huge birds that the birdwatchers had been so excited to find. Fred was telling the cats that hornbills make very loud throaty calls as they glide into the jungle canopy and that they eat ripe figs for breakfast. He also told the cats that the hornbills have a mating tree where they turn upside down to impress lady hornbills. Joey wanted to correct Fred and tell him it was the birds of paradise that turn upside down in their mating trees, but he decided not to hurt Fred's feelings. He doubted that the cats cared which bird turned upside down, anyway.

But not the humans! When the curator of the Harvard Museum of Natural History, which had sponsored the trip to the end of the world, saw Joey's picture in *National Geographic*, he threw a fit; he knew very well that Joey was just an ordinary house mouse and not any sort of rare "indigenous species" at all. He wrote a letter to *National Geographic* stating that Harvard had *extremely high principles*, and to make that sort of mistake about a new species on a trip sponsored by the Harvard Museum of Natural History was completely unacceptable. The editor of *National Geographic* replied tartly that the whole thing had been a mistake, that the photographer had been reprimanded, and that the next issue of the magazine was going to print an apology and a retraction—and would have done so without any letter from the curator.

Joey didn't feel a bit different after the retraction was printed. Most of the mice still regarded him as some sort of mouse celebrity, principally because of all of the fuss.

Joey was now forty-five mouse-years old. He had noticed, down at the farmhouse, a very nice young lady mouse named Emily. It seemed to Joey that he had never seen a mouse with such sparkling eyes, and when she brushed against him one evening as they passed in the china cupboard, he noted that her fur was very clean and had a wonderful smell.

He started to collect tiny bits of special food; for instance, he found a pignut hickory nut out in front of the farmhouse that still had a lot of the meat inside. He removed the remainder and carried it in to where he knew Emily would find it. Several days later, he was very nearly caught by a screech owl when he went out into the meadow after midnight, looking for fresh clover seeds for her. When she noticed that he was out of breath and all roughed up, she scolded him for taking such chances.

That was when Joey asked Emily if she would come up to the barn and see a nest he had built under a pile of old boards. He had been at it for some time; he had used a good bit of fur that Buck had rubbed off himself when he rolled on his back on the cement, trying to get rid of a deer tick. Joey had lined the nest with Kleenex he had taken from the box on Granny's dresser. He had even made two long trips down to the home of the policeman, where, in the pasture beside the house, he had collected a large ball of fur from his friend Ziggy, the alpaca. Finally, when the milkweed had dropped its pods and they had burst open and dried in the autumn air, Joey had gathered many of the fluffy seeds for a final inner lining. He thought it was a very fine nest.

So, late in the evening, when the grass was covered with heavy frost and there was a huge, full yellow moon shining, Joey and Emily crept from the farmhouse up to the old barn and slipped into the darkness. The motor home gleamed in its resting place as they hurried past. They darted around Buck, as he snored softly in a far corner, and slipped under the pile of old boards.

Emily looked the nest over very carefully. Then she inspected the three separate escape routes Joey had carefully prepared. She came

97

back to the nest and quietly told Joey that she had decided that she would move in. And, of course, they lived happily ever after.